WHEN SATAN CAME TO MOOSE LAKE

written by
Dewey Anderson

Copyright © 2007 by Dewey Anderson

When Satan Came to Moose Lake
by Dewey Anderson

Printed in the United States of America

ISBN 978-1-60477-086-5

All rights reserved solely by the author. The author guarantees all contents are original and do not infringe upon the legal rights of any other person or work. No part of this book may be reproduced in any form without the permission of the author. The views expressed in this book are not necessarily those of the publisher.

Unless otherwise indicated, Bible quotations are taken from the Revised Standard Version. Copyright © 1962 by A.J. Holman Company in Philadelphia.

www.xulonpress.com

CONTENTS

Preface vii
Acknowledgments ix
1. Looking Back 11
2. A Black Cloud 15
3. A Journey to the Ole Days 19
4. School Time 27
5. Upper Elementary Days 33
6. Christmas Vacation 41
7. Uncle Ozzie & Aunt Sophie 45
8. 4-H Days 51
9. Taking on the Farm 59
10. Army Days 67
11. Looking Back at Moose Lake 91
12. After the Army 97
13. Steel Plant Days 105
14. A Growing Black Cloud 113
15. Marriage & Family 121
16. The Split Rock Route 127
17. The Kettle River Route 133
18. Uncle Louis' Funeral 141
19. Allen 147
20. Satan Comes to Moose Lake 155

21. To Russia with Love 163
22. Farming for the Future 175
23. The Black Cloud Strikes in 1998 181
24. Raweana 185
25. Drug Test Results 191
26. Going to Drug Counseling 195
27. Snakes in the Grass 199
28. The Grant Writer 215
29. Missouri 219
30. The Trial Begins 225
31. Lawyers & the Illegal System 241
32. Lessons Learned 245
Epilogue 253

PREFACE

A friend of mine talked me into going to a young peoples' church supper. His girl friend would meet him there. They had been a strong item since high school.

Now we are in our middle 20's and I am looking for a farm girl. The Lord, I found works in mysterious ways.

I sat next to a college girl who told me she was on the Dean's List. She was a very cute young lady, wearing a white mini skirt and a flouncy top. I thought, boy if you can't stay out of trouble with this dean fellow, maybe I should stay away.

Well, my buddy's girl started hitting on me. I didn't want to offend him, but what can a young guy do? I knew the attention would be short lived but we took the short life and dated for a couple of weeks. At the same time, I dated this troubled college girl. She was a town girl which was not going to fit very well with farming.

I took her to the Dairy Queen for an ice cream cone. Well, she did the same thing there that she did at the church supper.

Suddenly, she slobbered all over the front of her white blouse. I was beginning to think maybe this was a girl that might need my help. We were married May 20, 1972.

I am proud to say GOD knew exactly what He was doing when He brought us together. Dianne and I can talk. We talk about everything and we also listen to each other.

She has been the most positive partner in the world. She has supported all of my farming adventures. She even bought the big Case tractor at an auction when I quit bidding because I thought it was too high priced.

She pulled me out of the mud an awful lot of times. She even helped with calving and pulled a calf by herself once when I was on a bus trip.

She graduated from Bemidji State College with an elementary teaching degree. Later she got a Masters Degree in Educational Media.

She is a fun person to be with and I miss her greatly when she has to go to work. She has a good sense of humor and a beautiful smile.

We have supported each other in good times and hard times. I could never be any happier with anyone but Dianne. She is a true gift from GOD.

Oh yeah, she also gave to me three sons that we are very proud of. Now we have three daughters-in-law that we love very much. We also have four grandchildren – they are great.

Before we were married, and ever since, we made a commitment to our Lord and Savior to trust and obey His Holy Word. We are not perfect but we ask Jesus to forgive our sins. He does and so it is with repentance of our sins that we will be in heaven with our Savior Jesus Christ.

~DEWEY P.S. I probably owe my wife of almost 36 years a trip to Hawaii, she's been hinting. So maybe if you buy my book, I can take her on a good vacation.

ACKNOWLEDGMENTS

After reading about the black cloud experiences, you might think I have a total negative attitude against all people. That is not true.

I will not name all the prayer partners involved in our situation. You know who you are and you have my gratitude. The many answers to prayers are phenomenal.

God has proven His greatness and power and love abundantly.

Thank you to the 700 Club and D. James Kennedy for prayer at key times before and during the court trial.

Thank you to those of you who gave money just in the nick of time to sustain our life. God really worked some miracles through you too.

Thank you to Sandy Lake Baptist Church and Stone Bluff Methodist Church of Indiana for sustaining us with your prayers.

I could not have done this book without the encouragement from my wife. This was several years in the making. Reliving the events of the hardest part of our lives was almost impossible and very painful to do.

There was an almost constant nagging in my heart and soul to write this book. I think this nagging came from God. Thank you, God.

During the difficult years waiting for the trial, God graciously gave a new business idea. I had to start a new career in the business world. I learned how to make soybean candles.

Also thank you to all who supported me and my family.

Thank you for buying the book. Please tell everyone you know to buy it. If you would like a speaker at your church or club or civic organization just e-mail us at showmecountrygifts@yahoo.com.

- 1 -

LOOKING BACK

It was going to be another sunny, warm, spring day in May. The man had gotten up early as was his usual custom. These early mornings were a nice quiet time to read and check the e-mails. It was a good time to think.

Today would probably be a good day to begin haying the first crop. Spring had brought with it both much needed moisture and plenty of warm days. Which field to start on was always an important question. This would be a good time to take a last look at the west field to be sure that was really the right one. So off he went.

As he stood in the field, he noticed that the alfalfa and clover had declined somewhat again. It was so hard to keep a good crop. If you did not have sufficient snow fall, you would have more grass and less of what the cows liked the best. The previous winter had obviously taken its toll. The cold weather had come at the usual time. However, significant snow had not arrived until February this year. It would still be a good crop, but it should have been a bit better. Winter in northern Minnesota was often hard on crops, animals, and people as well.

The man turned to look north. There was that northeast field. It had started out some thirty five years ago as a willow infested swampy area. He had worked for years on that field to get it into production. Plowing, seeding, fertilizing furiously only to have it say "thank you" by giving a short, shrimpy, sparse yield. But God, the Father had been watching the toil and finally the effort had paid off. What he saw now was a lush and green field. It would also soon be ready for haying.

Every year, he wondered if this would be the year he would find his wrench. Many years before, he had lost a 12 inch crescent wrench. At that time, the field was so bumpy the wrench slid off the tractor. Several times he had walked the field in hopes of finding the wrench. Perhaps the wrench had worked its way to the other side of the world by this time. Well, one thing was for sure – today was not going to be the day he found his wrench.

Just behind this field was his pasture. He smiled as he remembered some of the cows and calves he had raised over the years. There was Lop Eye and Lop Ear. They had made quite a pair. Beautiful and black, they each had just that one little flaw. Then there was Ralpherd. The boys had named her. She was one strange looking cow. She had a short stumpy body with a gigantic head. Ralpherd had a great personality. In fact, when prospective buyers came to look over the herd, Ralpherd was always front and center.

One of his favorite things had been to sit on a stump in the middle of the animals and wait for them to come to him. Many of the cows had just looked at him as if to say, "Oh, it's just him." But the calves were a different story. They were curious. The brave ones would slowly creep up. Sniffing, they would check to see what kind of calf he was. The really "brave" ones were the ones approaching from behind. Soon the man would feel their breath on his neck and then a lick from one of them. This always brought a smile to his face. Could he pet them today? As he lifted his hand to touch one, the fearful ones would flee for their lives. The others stayed and accepted the coveted pat on the head and the scratches behind their ears. Oh, how the man longed for those days. But the "travesty" had ended all of that.

Turning to the west, the man surveyed the neighborhood. Memories of both good and not-so-good came to him. There were so many haying memories from past years that came. The breakdowns always came at the most inconvenient times. The hay crops were often beyond his expectations. God was good! He remembered the lunches that had been eaten out on the field with his wife and boys. They always came about the time he thought he was going to pass out from starvation.

Today, he had a lot of ground to cover. One memory he hoped would not appear today was weather related. On this field it was easy to see the approaching storms. He would work feverishly to finish the haying before that dark cloud arrived. Then suddenly he would see the wall of rain approaching. Run! Run for cover. No matter how fast he ran, he would get drenched. He hoped today would not be like that.

The south brought memories of its own. The tragic loss of a neighbor's child brought sadness all over again. Many neighbors had come and gone. Very few of the new ones seemed interested in getting to know anyone else. It definitely was not like the "good old days" when neighbors visited and got to know each other. They had become wonderful friends. It was different now. People seemed colder and more uncaring.

The south also brought visions of the little place he had for three years in Missouri. That little move had not been in the plans. It was the "travesty" that caused it. Reflecting back on that time for a moment, he realized again that God had definitely used what Satan meant for evil and turned it into something good. You could count on God for things like that.

Well, it was time to get busy. As the man turned to the east, he looked up. There it was again. He never used to be able to see it. But since the "travesty" he could see it more and more often. This was a bright sunshine day. There were no clouds to be seen as he gazed up at the sky. That is, except for that dark, ominous, black cloud that hung over the town of Moose Lake.

- 2 -

A BLACK CLOUD

The man had noticed that the black cloud was visible to him nearly every day now. It was a strange cloud. It would appear even if the sky was completely clear. He could not tell if it was imagination or not, but the cloud seemed to be getting bigger.

He had discovered some time ago that not everyone could see the cloud. In fact, he was able to see the cloud only after the "travesty". Before that time, he only knew about the cloud from others who were able to see it.

There were many outsiders who said that they saw a black cloud over Moose Lake. These people were adamant about seeing the cloud. They emphatically said they would drive many miles out of their way to go around Moose Lake. The cloud gave them a terrifying feeling the closer they got to Moose Lake. This feeling was oppressive and they were very concerned about the people of little Moose Lake.

One thing that was most amazing was that none of these people knew each other. In fact, some of these people really were strangers to the man himself.

The man remembered asking these people what the cloud was all about. Their response was always very similar. They all agreed that the cloud was evil. This answer was very disturbing to him.

They tried to explain to him that the cloud had not always existed. You see, Moose Lake started out as a quiet, sleepy, little town like most rural towns. They could not tell exactly when the cloud first appeared because the first time any of them had noticed it, the cloud was no more than a tiny wisp in the sky that seemed out of place.

As they considered the history of the little town, they had realized that the cloud seemed to become more noticeable as the town changed some of its moral standings. They said the cloud reflected the moral choices of the townspeople.

Early on, the people of Moose Lake were devoted, church going, Bible believing people. They worked hard, were close to their neighbors, and closer to God. But the saying "all good things must come to an end" seemed to have come true.

The size of the black cloud was supposedly related to the level of evil being "winked at" by the good people of Moose Lake. At first the cloud was small when the evil was more limited. For instance, during the fifties and early sixties several prestigious couples in Moose Lake participated in what was called the "Key Club".

There were several rumors about how this little group worked. The most prevalent scenario went something like this: several couples would meet for an evening of socializing. They would put their car keys on the table. When it was time to go home, the wives would take the keys of the man they wanted to go home with. The rumor mill had it that Moose Lake was getting to be a regular little Peyton Place.

As the man thought back to what the people had told him about the black cloud, he wondered how he could have been so blind and not seen the cloud much earlier than he did.

Certainly, he had seen over the years, the changes in his little community. Sometimes it would seem that one cannot see or understand evil until it visits your own doorstep.

Enough of this. Evil of this magnitude had not always existed in this little town and the man had not always been a man.

- 3 -

A JOURNEY TO THE GOOD 'OLE DAYS

It was a bright, spring day in April, 1944 that a little boy, named Dewey was born. He was the youngest of the eight children that were born to a very traditional Norwegian family.

There was guarded excitement about the arrival of this new little one. You see, the couple's oldest son had been born healthy too. However, he had died of leukemia at six years of age. Can you imagine the feelings that a young couple would have when their little one died so young? The most difficult thing for any parent is to bury their children. It just does not seem right. During that time, a lot of young children died of various illnesses. Doctors in those days did not have all the information and equipment for analysis and diagnosis of diseases like doctors have today.

All together, there were four boys and four girls born in this family. After the experience they had with their first one, it was very difficult to look at each of their children as they arrived and wonder just how long this child would survive. They learned not to take anything for granted. Life can change so quickly.

The family lived on a dairy farm just outside of Moose Lake. It took a lot of hard work and ingenuity to make ends meet. Everything was done by hand as they had no modern conveniences.

Moose Lake in the 1940s and 50s, like all of America, was trying to get over the effects of the 1930s Depression and World War II which left a real hard mark on the American people.

Many of the rich that lost everything killed themselves. They saw no hope. They put all their value into monetary things. They could not stand losing their power and money. It was horrible for them.

So maybe the lesson was, if you are poor don't worry about it. If things go "south", you don't have much to lose. Remember what the Bible says? "It is easier for a camel to go through the eye of a needle than for a rich man to enter the kingdom of God." (Matthew 19:24)

Being the youngest child, his "big" sisters all felt they needed to raise him up right. So they took on the task of correcting his every move. Of course, this included the usual sisterly teasing that is needed to "train up a boy in the way he should go."

As Dewey grew up, he began helping with the usual farm chores expected of farm kids. He observed everything around him and as all little boys, he wondered what made things work.

One hot July day, his Dad was very busy trying to make hay before the rain came. It was always a challenge to get the hay done before rain came.

However, in those days, the Norwegian traditions of meal time stood no matter what was happening. That included haying season too.

When Satan Came to Moose Lake

The day started with milking and feeding the cows at five o'clock each morning. After that was done, the family was served by his Mom a big breakfast meal including bacon, eggs, toast with jelly, and milk straight from the cow. Everything on the farm was home grown and homemade.

Around mid-morning, it was coffee time in most Norwegian households. However, since Dad had his milk route, the family did not have this ten o'clock meal. They worked straight through to dinner.

At dinner time, which was at noon, work again stopped and the family was delighted to find a very hearty meal waiting for them. This meal always included meat, potatoes, a vegetable like peas, carrots, corn, radishes or lettuce from the garden, and desert.

There is much controversy today about what this meal should be called. On the farm, the meal took place at noon and was a hefty one. It was called dinner. People nowadays call it lunch, but at that time, lunch was what you had between the main meals of breakfast, dinner, and supper. It would be more like what we call a "snack" today.

Yes, you guessed it. In the middle of the afternoon it was coffee time again. This was always welcome in the summer, as it meant a time to get out of the hot sun and get refreshed. It was something to keep you going until supper. Coffee was always served. The kids were never allowed to have coffee, they always had milk. Coffee was a "grown up" drink.

Supper time was not to be out done by any of the other meals of the day. Meat, potatoes, and desert kept everyone going so they could finish the chores of the day. Meat consisted of beef, pork, or chickens that had all been raised on the farm. They especially liked the steaks and roasts. All this cooking kept Dewey's Mom very busy.

Everyone that came to her house was treated like royalty with some of the best Norwegian cooking in the county. She always took good care of all who were at her table during meal time and coffee time.

Her strawberry patch was probably one of the best in the county. She raised Ogalala strawberries. They even had to stop haying one day to pick the berries before they got too ripe. They had the basement floor covered with berries waiting to be processed. His Mom made lots of jam, jelly, and sauce for the family.

Every day during strawberry season, she would make baking powder biscuits. Then they would get strawberry shortcake with real whipped cream. They could have all the strawberries on their shortcakes that they wanted as long as they picked more the next day.

Feeding you was one of the ways that she told you that she loved you. Words of affection were not shared. You knew you were cared for by the things she provided for you such as food, clothing, and taking care of the house. To her these were acts of love.

It was during one of these dinner meals that Dewey's curiosity got the best of him. His Dad had stopped to eat and was going right out to the field to finish up the haying before the rain came.

Little boys are always wondering how things fit together and how they work. Today was no exception. With wrench in hand, Dewey went to work to take the hay bucker apart.

By the time his father was ready to go back to the field, Dewey had very successfully dismantled the hay bucker.

To say his Dad was not happy would be an understatement. But in his traditional, quiet Norwegian way, he just put it back together and finally finished the haying that day. He was also, much more careful about where he left his wrenches after that.

In his mind, he was also proud of his little five year old son for being so able to take the hay bucker apart. He only hoped that when the child got older, he would also be able to put things back together again!

Being raised on the farm gave Dewey many wonderful experiences. One day one of the neighbor's sheep wandered into their yard. Five year old Dewey was not about to let this go without some excitement. He leaped on the back of the wooly creature and hung on. The sheep decided to take him for a quick ride across the yard. It was a great big Shropshire. That was the breed of choice back in the thirties and forties.

After the war, there was much demand for food, especially vegetables. His father contracted with the canning company to raise beans. By doing this he helped feed the country and help his family make ends meet. They raised five acres of green beans. When the beans needed picking and weeding, sometimes it seemed like the rows went on for miles. Every bean plant was picked and weeded completely by hand. Each of the kids helped pick the beans so they would be ready when the truck came to get them.

When the truck came, it was the biggest truck Dewey had ever seen. The man driving the truck was always in a hurry because the beans had to get to the factory for canning. Each of the bags were made of canvas and had to be filled just right. The bags were about five feet long. The trucker had a scale to weigh the bags of beans. His Dad was paid by the pound for the beans.

When Dewey was five years old, he also learned how to drive tractor. At least, he learned how to steer. It was much easier to have him drive the tractor and wagon so his Dad and brother could pick up the hay piles on each side of the wagon and fork them on. There were four slings on the wagon. That would be four hay loads that would go up into the hay mow. The tractor he drove was a small one. It was a John Deere LA. His Dad was very proud of that tractor and his son. They had both arrived on the farm, brand new, in 1944.

During these years, his Dad provided Moose Lake cafes, restaurants, and homes with fresh milk, cream, and butter. That meant he was away from home a lot. Since this was a dairy farm, the family all needed to milk the cows, feed them, and clean the barn.

Dewey always enjoyed working with animals, so he enjoyed his time milking the cows. With all of the cows named, he took care of them like they were part of the family.

When he was about fourteen, he was the one who took over most of the farming. By this time, all of the other kids had grown up and left the farm. Summer was especially difficult because in addition to getting up and doing the milking, feeding, and barn cleaning at five o'clock, there was the haying to do. Often it got to the point where he thought he would not be able to keep going.

It was about that time that his other older brother would show up. His brother worked in the mines. If he was able, he would finish work on Friday and come down to the farm to help out.

Dewey really looked up to his brother. He was about ten years older than him. He thought there was nothing his big brother could not do. So when his brother arrived, it gave him just the added energy he needed to get the task done. It was wonderful to have a brother like that.

The family did not go out into the community very often. One of the sons, who was about eight years older than Dewey, was profoundly handicapped. It was difficult for the family to go anywhere because of the snickers, stares, and mean comments that were made. There was no acceptance for those with disabilities in those days. People can be so mean. It was just easier for the family to stay home than to put up with the meanness.

The family had a hard life on the farm. But they had no idea what an easy life was so it did not make any difference.

His Dad and Mom worked the kids all hard so they could do the same for their own family some day. A good work ethic was considered essential in those days. Laziness was not tolerated.

Between working on the farm and going to school, Dewey was always kept very busy.

- 4 -

SCHOOL TIME

For the most part, Dewey had a good education at Moose Lake. He had very good teachers. To this day he calls them "million dollar teachers".

That is except for Mrs. Grace. She was only ten cents worth. She was his third grade teacher. He did not know of anyone who liked her. Especially the eight classmates she failed did not like her. It is amazing but every one she failed that year went on to excel in life despite her two years of demeaning, condemning, harassing, and teasing. She would tease about a scar or how ugly you looked.

If you got wet pants from playing in the snow you had to take your pants off in front of the class and hang them on the hot water radiator to dry. While you were hanging your pants up, Mrs. Grace led the class in hysterical laughter. When the girls got wet pants, they never had to take their pants off.

One time Gary dared question Mrs. "Disgrace" (that is what the students called her behind her back). She got so mad at him she was going to make him go pure naked. That was too much for little Gary to take. He ran out of the room and headed for home. Mrs. Grace made great threats to the whole class, for surely we would never see Gary again.

Apparently, Mrs. Grace did not know that Gary's father was the school board chairman. The kids assumed Gary's dad had a little clout over Mrs. "Disgrace". They never had to pull their pants down again. Two of the guys were really thankful because in those days, some of the parents could not afford underwear or what they had was filled with holes. Nowadays, the "Brittney Spear's" thing does not seem to bother anybody. How times have changed.

As with all kids, some classes were easy and some were very difficult. Reading and spelling were his best and most favorite subjects. Adventure stories were the kind of story he liked the best. They used to get the Weekly Reader. He liked reading the stories about different parts of the world. He loved pictures of different animals from around the world.

He looked forward to recess time. In the winter, students could go skating. They had a nice hockey rink down by the lake. There was a tar paper shack with a wood stove. Axel was the caretaker of the park and the skating rink. He kept the snow shoveled off the rink. At times the boys would help him get the snow off. If there was a lot of snow, Dewey's Dad would come down with his John Deere MT and plow the snow off the rink. Axel was an old time pioneer of Moose Lake. He was nice but very strict. He did this as volunteer work in his retirement.

The first day of third grade did not start out well. They were all out playing behind the school before school started. One of the boys, Mike, started beating on a cocker spaniel. He would not stop. The dog was yelping in terrible pain. Mike was beating and kicking the dog until the dog was nearly unconscious.

Dewey ran over and started beating Mike up. He got him down to the ground. They were rolling and punching.

Mike was crying and gave up. He went in the school house crying.

Dewey came in later. Both he and Mike were greatly reprimanded by Mrs. Disgrace. They both had come to school in nice clean clothes and after that bout, they were all dirty and rumpled up. What a mess they were! Mike had somehow gotten a cut lip.

About an hour later, over the intercom came the order for Dewey to go to the Superintendent's office. Boy was he scared then. He had thought the whole thing was all over, but it wasn't.

Mr. Doocken told him that Dewey had started a big fight with Mike and had broken his glasses. He told Mr. Doocken that Mike did not have glasses on during the fight. He asked Dewey why he had started a fight with Mike. He told him that Mike was beating up on a little dog in the school yard. The poor dog was yelping with pain and he was afraid Mike was going to kill the dog.

Mr. Doocken asked how big the dog was. Dewey showed him that it was just a little dog. Then he asked him what color it was.

"Black", said Dewey.

"Do you know what kind it was?" he asked.

Dewey answered, "I think it was a cocker spaniel."

Mr. Doocken told him thank you and dismissed him to go back to class.

Dewey found out later that the dog Mike was beating up belonged to the Superintendent's family. Mike got into real big trouble and had to pay for his own glasses! Mike never liked Dewey after that.

Dewey did not like Math or Science. He liked Geography even though he did not understand it all that well. Science was so boring back then. It was just reading about the concepts. It was not a hands-on- learning experience.

Another one of Dewey's favorite subjects was Lunch! Chili was his day. They had real good cooks. They made the best chili in the world. If you were nice, they would give seconds. This was generally not allowed.

Besides the learning that he had at school, Dewey had to go to Sunday School every Sunday. He would rather have stayed home and played on the farm. Anything, so he would not have to go to school of any kind. He loved being outside.

Dewey figured that it was in elementary school that his Alzheimer's really began.(Just kidding!) He had such a difficult time memorizing things. That made Sunday School very difficult because he was always having to memorize Bible verses.

Christmas programs were also difficult. Back in those days, kids were given a "piece" that they had to learn. It was always incredibly long and difficult. They did not let anyone use cue cards. You better learn it or there would be trouble at home.

He remembered one Christmas program in particular. The Sunday School Superintendent was Mrs. Doocken, wife to the public school Superintendent. She had decided that her son, Billy, and Dewey should say their parts together. Billy was a real cry baby. He was always dressed in nice clothes because his parents were the richest people in town.

Dewey had a terrible time memorizing his "piece". In fact, he was only able to memorize the first half. As the kids were standing on the stairway waiting to go on stage, Dewey turned to Billy who was behind him.

He said, "I will do the first half and you do the second half."

Billy indignantly said, "That's not what my mother said to do."

Dewey repeated what he said and added, "You'll do as I say and say the second half or else!"

The boys went on stage and did their "piece" just as Dewey had said. Mrs. Doocken was horrified with the change in her program. During the lunch in the Church basement after the program, Billy's mom just glared at Dewey. He suspected that cry baby Billy had told his mom what all Dewey had said.

Dewey had lots of memories of school. After all he was there for twelve years! They were smart enough in those days that kids did not need kindergarten.

- 5 -

UPPER ELEMENTARY DAYS

One of the nicest teachers in the world had her hands full. She was a great teacher because she knew how to handle any situation. She laid things out for the students and gave them choices. One of them happened when he was in the 4th grade. Something struck him and the other boys. It was a phenomenon. It hit all of them.

Looking back, Dewey did not know how their teacher taught them anything. The boys had no concentration, except for girls. The girls had no concentration except for the boys. It did not last all that long. Crushes lasted a week or two.

All of a sudden, the girls they had known for at least the last four years just seemed to look pretty to them.

Their hair was combed and soft and clean. They wore such pretty dresses, no make up or jewelry. It was just pure beauty.

Someone got brave and passed a love note. Back then, if a girl looked at a boy it meant she loved him.

Dicky always had lots of looks so he could have four or five girl friends at one time. Dicky was so cute, and he could handle all those girls with such finesse. He had the nicest smile and the girls loved his sweet smile.

Dewey marveled at Dicky and all his girl friends. He had some resentment for Dicky's natural abilities with the girls. You kind of wanted to be in the loop with Dicky.

Usually a girl's look only lasted a week at most. You had to pay attention to the girls in case a girl looked at you, so you did not miss her attention. As a young boy, learning about girls at such a young age was traumatic at best. In later years it became terrifying!

One day there were so many notes being passed in the underground note passing railroad, that some of the notes fell into the wrong hands. The boys were confused and the girls were mad.

At one point it made more noise than the teacher's chalk scratching on the blackboard.

Miss Johnson was the kindest teacher in the world. She was so understanding and so smart. The students considered her one of their best teachers. They all loved her very much. They even begged her to be their teacher for the 5th grade, too.

Miss Johnson never married. Dewey guessed she had more time and effort to give to her students because of that. Teachers barely made a living in those days. He remembered how Miss Johnson used her own money for picnics and a treat once in a while.

Well, Miss Johnson caught the students at the worst possible time. It was right at the height of note passing. Dewey believed she knew all along what was going on but pretended not to know so she could catch them all at the same time. Wow! She was smart.

Suddenly they heard, "All right. Bring all the notes to my desk. Come on. You too. Hurry up!"

There was quite a stack of them on her desk. Some were rolled up real small. Others were folded over ever so carefully. Some of the notes had the recipients name on the front. A few notes fell to the floor and no one dared pick them up for fear Miss Johnson would see them bend over for it.

As scared as they were for getting caught, it was not a fear of their teacher that filled them. It was a fear of what she would do with the notes. You see, at the height of this note making adventure, things got very steamy in those little notes. It could prove to be very humiliating and embarrassing should any one read these little manuscripts of love.

Miss Johnson did not have a mean bone in her body. But at that moment of time, something made her break from the monotony of repetition and try some thing different.

She made it look like this situation was a real good teaching assignment. She made it look as if they had turned in extra credit papers.

Here is how it went. She was serious but kind. She said, "Well class, what shall I do with all these letters?"

The students were stunned to think she was giving them the chance to make a monumental decision like that. This was a decision that would affect their existence for the rest of their lives.

Ah! But before they could think, Miss Johnson was way ahead of them as usual. She said, "You can throw them in the garbage." There was a big garbage can that sat at the end of her desk.

A flash of hope came across the class room. It was a saving grace to forth graders. They were being saved by the bell. It was a reprieve from Miss Johnson.

Then she continued, "Or you can read them out loud so we can all learn about sentence structure, grammar, and spelling."

The room suddenly warmed up to four hundred degrees on that cold winter day. The girls were incensed that their personal lives would be opened to the public. They would never be able to come to school again.

Everyone's face turned red as she said, "Let the reading begin." There was such silence it was deafening.

"Who's would be first?"

"Did I sign my name?"

"Oh please bring those letters that fell on the floor." Miss Johnson said. "We don't want to miss any, do we?"

No one worried about Dicky's feelings because he liked attention, any attention.

It was some pretty steamy stuff even for back in 1953.

She began to read. "You want to play marbles with me? I like you. Do you like me? Yes or No."

"Oh, someone forgot to put his name on this one. Who wrote this one?"

Miss Johnson complimented everyone on how nice the letters were. She asked if they would all like to write a whole page about someone in the class for an assignment. There were many moans and groans about that. The students had just had enough embarrassment to last a long time.

Or would they rather have a math assignment? A cheer went up and note passing in the 4th grade was a milestone that was now in the past and not to happen again, until fifth grade.

Fifth grade brought a wonderful surprise. Miss Johnson also graduated from the fourth grade and was now their fifth grade teacher.

The boys did a lot of ice skating and Dewey had no clue what the girls did that year. Were they there???

The students learned a lot that year. It was really an uneventful year. Unless learning is eventful.

Grade six gave Dewey and his classmates another wonderful teacher. Her name was Mrs. Kjarum.

The class stayed basically the same all twelve years of school. There were about forty-eight kids in their class. They knew each other fairly well.

Dewey discovered that a national holiday was a poor time to get the look from a girl. Christmas and Valentine's Day were especially bad.

Dewey's class always made Valentine boxes. They were decorated real fancy and colorful. If you wanted lots of Valentine cards you made a big box.

On the big day everyone had such big hopes for getting a special Valentine from a special person. It never happened the way they had hoped.

Guys were easily swayed. The girls were different.

Wouldn't you know! In sixth grade, Dewey got the look. It was from Lois. She was a new kid. She was very out going. When she passed notes, she hoped they would get intercepted. He thought maybe she was starved for attention.

The look began around Christmas of 1954. If you get a girl friend at a holiday you have to get her a nice present.

Dewey went up town at noon hour one day. He went to the Ben Franklin and shopped to the last minute. He finally settled for a pen set mainly because it was in a box and it was small. He would be able to hide it.

He really was not enthralled with Lois. She was so pushy and that embarrassed him. **Just breathing embarrassed him in those young years!**

Really, all he wanted for extra curricular activities at the time was 4-H and the Smoky the Bear Club. He wanted to prevent forest fires and keep the earth clean. He believed strongly in conservation. He wanted to grow up to be a forest ranger.

But first he had to get the Christmas gift to Lois before the end of the day because Christmas vacation would soon begin. If he did not get it to her quickly he would not see her until next year.

After they ate dinner (and by the way, dinner was at noon in the old days and supper was at 6 p.m.) he got Lois to go outside.

She was loud and full of questions. "Where are we going? Do you have something for me?" Lois had been strongly hinting and harping about a present for a week. He just wanted to get her far away from everyone so she could not embarrass him. But she wanted to be in the public eye.

They headed for the lake. No, he wasn't gonna drown her! He couldn't even if he wanted to because the lake was frozen over with three feet of ice.

Lois just kept on with her prattle. "Can I have it now? What did you get me?"

Well, it felt like half the school followed them to the lake. So Dewey just kept going. Boy it was cold. The wind out there was blowing snow and making whirlwinds. The snow was about ten inches deep.

Finally he got Lois to the middle of Moose Head Lake. He handed her the nicely wrapped present. She took it and ripped the wrapping and the cover off and flagrantly tossed them on the ice and snow causing an irrevocable environmental pollution of a horrific magnitude!

He was devastated. Lois was ecstatic. She hugged him. He saw it coming and just in time he turned his face to catch the kiss on his cheek.

Well, we better get back he thought. He ran after the environmental spill and got that cleaned up. She asked why he was bothering with that.

He could not wait for Christmas vacation. When they got back to school they were a few minutes late. Lois burst into the classroom telling Mrs. Kjarum and the whole class "Look what Dewey gave me for Christmas." She was so excited, so happy, so obnoxious.

Dewey put the wrappings in the paper receptacle and proceeded to die.

Many times Mrs. Kjarum saw the story unfold and he assumed she figured he suffered enough so being late for class was forgiven. He remembered her big smirk between the guffaws of his classmates. The end of the day could not come soon enough. But finally, the last bus ride home for that year came. Ahh!! Safe at home on vacation at last!

- 6 -

CHRISTMAS VACATION

Winters were hard on the farm. They always had to get more wood for the furnace. The winters were harsh. Just keeping everything thawed out was a full time job with cows to milk, calves to feed, barn cleaning, and pitching hay.

Everything was done by hand so his parents needed all the help they could get. They always got Sunday off because GOD said people needed a day of rest. Just about everyone rested on Sunday. You still had to milk, clean, and feed though. That's farming Dewey remembered one Sunday when they were all in the living room. The sun was out so bright. It was about two o'clock in the afternoon.

The wind was very brisk and it was really cold out. His sister spotted someone walking on the highway. They all wondered who would be out walking on a day like this. Maybe their car broke down. Or maybe they slid in the ditch.

The whole family was soon at the big triple windows on the south side of the house. His Mom said "It looks like a young girl."

Someone else said, "Well I hope she don't freeze out there. I wonder where she is going. Oh look! She's coming in our driveway. She's coming to the house. She's probably freezing cold and needs a place to get warmed up. "

Dewey recognized her coat and scarf. As she got close, they all asked him if he knew who it was. It was as if it was somehow Dewey's fault that someone was braving the elements to enter our domain. It was Lois!

They told Dewey to go to the door. There was always a big argument in his home about who should go to the door. No one wanted to answer the door. Maybe that's why they did not have much company.

Everyone in the family was embarrassed about seeing or talking to anyone. What a dumb way to be!

The biggest problem Dewey's whole family had was that they did not know how to communicate. They had no idea how to express sadness because crying and things like that were considered to be a show of weakness. A good full blooded Norwegian does not show weakness, excitement, or jubilation.

The home was run with strict discipline. Do not talk at meal time or you would get the look. The look came from Dad. His Mom had a look too, but not like Dad. It was like he could see into you. He never laid a hand on any one. He did not need to. He could dissect your bad behavior from where he sat. You could melt into a puddle even if it was forty below zero if Dad gave the look.

Both his Mom and Dad had eyes in the back of their heads. There was never ever a four letter word said. Even the word "darn" was prohibited. The flip side of that was that the other four letter words were never used either. You know, words like love. Love came from doing for each other, not talking about it.

Their fore fathers had so much turmoil in their lives just to stay alive; worrying about feelings was the last thing they were concerned about. The Great Depression of the thirties defined the attitudes of most Americans.

Most families were large. Having from six to twenty-two children in a family was fairly common. It left little time or energy for dialog and feelings assessment.

If a person had a problem, he was expected to just buck up and fix it. It made good strong individuals. It made good patriots to serve the country when war came. They did not have flag burners then. If there had been any, they would be tried for treason. People had a love for GOD, family, country, the flag, prayer in school, and the Ten Commandments. It worked well then and it could work now.

Today's children are not allowed to pray in school. That is one of the reasons why kids now are so dumb in school.

What Dewey needed now was prayer. Lois was at the door. He ran upstairs and prepared to die.

He heard his sisters invite Lois in. She thanked them for coming to the door and started saying what a beautiful house they had.

His asked who she was.

"I'm Lois. I came to see Dewey. Is he home?"

"Please tell her Dewey died." he prayed. "Pleeeeese. Things are really tough on the farm today."

But what did he hear instead? "Dewey, Dewey, someone's here to see you." He thought maybe I didn't really hear that. But there it was again! "Dewey, Lois is here with a Christmas present."

Who would not want a Christmas gift when you are so poor you are lucky to get one pair of shoes in three years? He always got hand me downs and it was unusual to have a shoe with out a hole in it.

So what did Lois have in store for him? She had walked three miles from her home in the bitter cold to give him a present. He reluctantly came down the stairway to meet Miss Lois, exuberant as always.

Lois, Dewey later found out, was a foster child and was sent to many homes. She was never able to settle in one place very long. She was a very nice girl and he often wondered whatever happened to her. She did not finish the school year. She was gone.

But for now, she was standing eyeball to eyeball with him putting a gift in his hands. The whole family encircled them as if to attack in case there was something to eat.

Dewey very carefully, cautiously, slowly unwrapped the box. He was not quick enough, so Lois started helping him.

Oh, great! He thought, "I don't even know how to unwrap a present."

In his family they always saved the wrapping paper and reused it over and over. But not Lois. He wondered where in the world had she come from. Was she rich or what?

Lois was so excited to give him a gift. She went into such exaggerations about his taking her to the middle of the lake and giving her a pen set that she would cherish the rest of her life. The pen set cost fifty cents.

Lois finally let him open the box, but she took the object out and wrapped it around his neck. Oh good, he thought. "Strangle me in front of my whole family".

It was a beautiful knit scarf. She told them all that since Dewey had been so nice to give her the best gift ever; she wanted to give him something. It had taken her several days to knit but she did it herself.

It took everything he had to hold the tears back. What an act of kindness. And to think she walked three miles for him.

As Dewey reminisced, he realized that he still appreciated the memory of you, Lois. If he saw you now, he would give you a big hug. "We wouldn't have to go to the middle of the lake, and a kiss on the cheek too." The scarf really was beautiful, warm, and colorful.

- 7 -

UNCLE OZZY & AUNT SOPHIE

One of Dewey's favorite memories involved his Aunt Sophie. She was his mother's sister.

Back in the 1940's and 50's many farm families left the land for employment in the big city. So there were many vacant farms in the area.

When Dewey was eight years old (that would be in 1952), he and his sister would walk to a vacant farm and explore. She would make up ghost stories about this or that place.

They always went on these excursions in the evening. As the sun was setting, a little breeze would make those old farm buildings creeeeek and groan. For an eight year old it was a lot of trauma even for those days. But it was exhilarating. It was exciting.

Along the fence line they would find wild June berries and raspberries. They were really good eating. Sometimes if they had a pail they would pick enough for a June berry pie, which is the best pie in the world. Wild raspberries make the best jam.

Looking back fifty years, you could walk right into an abandoned house and barn. In those days no one locked their doors. Some homes were even left with the furnishings.

Since Dewey was the youngest in the family, it seemed that teasing him was a requirement. He got it from all of his sisters and brothers. The next kid in age to him was his sister who was six years older.

His brothers and sisters also held a great fear factor over him. He did not dare tell his Mom and Dad about anything they did. He was basically raised by his sisters. To them, Dewey did not dress correctly. They told him he did not eat right, "Eat with your mouth shut. Don't talk with your mouth full, say please pass the beans."

He did not walk correctly either. They would say, "Pick up your feet when you walk."

Eight years old and he could not eat, sleep, walk, dress, talk, or "breeeeeth" correctly. Some said that's why his siblings moved out of town when they graduated from school.

Anyway, one warm evening Dewey and his sister took a walk on a country road about two miles down a dead end road. It was barely a cow path, with tall grass grown up. But Sis said, "Uncle Ozzy and Aunt Sophie's farm is out here." So off they went.

It was a big old house with lots of large trees for shade. There was an apple orchard. Almost everyone planted orchards in those days. Some plums were ripe, so they ate them.

They were cautious about going in that house even though they knew no one was around. They whispered. "You open the door." Sis would say. Dewey wanted to be brave but he knew Uncle Ozzy and he was a little afraid of him.

Uncle Ozzy had a different kind of a voice than anyone had ever heard then or now. It was a gruff voice with a deep Scandinavian accent. But he seemed to have to strain to get the words out. He was always in such a heavy turmoil. There always seemed to be a crisis in his life. As Dewey got older, he could understand Uncle Ozzie's feelings.

The sun was setting and on a late summer evening there was still enough light for them to get home. They just had to get inside and explore.

Sis went first. As they crept in, they expected someone or something to come around the corner any time. Dewey could not resist the temptation, so he goosed his sister. Sis screamed so loud she would have scared ghosts away.

Uncle Ozzy and Aunt Sophie had vacated the farm several years earlier in the late 1940s. They took their four children to Duluth.

There Uncle Ozzy found work at the United States Steel Mill in Morgan Park. Uncle Ozzy did very well at USS. He made good money as well he had to. The farm was barely subsistence living and Aunt Sophie could not live the farm life.

So after Sis recovered from the goosing, they went in through the open door. The two kids looked at all the furniture that was left. Even the stove and electric refrigerator were still there.

It was getting dark in the house now. All the trees covering the outside of the house, kept the light from coming in.

Dewey and Sis joked about just turning the light on. Being the obedient brother that he was, he turned the light switch on.

They could not believe it. The lights came on. The power company must have forgotten about this remote place. Even the fuse box had been left. A person could have set up house keeping. Just bring food!

Thinking about his adventure with Sis brought to mind a bit more about Uncle Ozzie and Aunt Sophie.

Uncle Ozzy needed a good paying job. Aunt Sophie said one time, "It is Ozzy's job to make the money. It is my job to spend it." And she did!

Aunt Sophie was the youngest of twelve on Dewey's Mom's side of the family. Aunt Sophie was very flamboyant. She always wore a smile. She always wanted to do something exciting. She was the total opposite of Dewey's Mom and Dad.

Aunt Sophie dressed immaculately. She always wore a beautiful dress, earrings, a necklace, and lipstick that would leave a lip print on each cheek when she chased Dewey down and caught him and planted one on his cheek.

Dewey was so shy and embarrassed at any attention back then. He had to admit he kind of liked it now!

Sophie's two daughters were the most beautiful girls in the world. They would chase Dewey down until they caught him and tickle him mercilessly so he could not breathe. Then they would resuscitate him with kisses.

When Aunt Sophie and Uncle Ozzy came to visit it was the same rhetoric. "Sophie spends too much!" Uncle Ozzy would tell all the stuff she bought that week and if he forgot something, she would remind him.

Uncle Ozzy would get so worked up that pretty soon he would be just hollering. It really was comical because Aunt Sophie always had a smile on her face about everything Uncle Ozzy said. It seemed she was proud to hear of her accomplishments.

Then she would say, "Well Ozzy, if you are so worried we won't have enough money, why don't you just get another job?"

So it started all over again. Uncle Ozzy would reply, "I already work sixteen hours a day. You want me to live at work?" On and on it went.

When they went some place, Aunt Sophie had to drive because Uncle Ozzy drove too slowly for her.

When Satan Came to Moose Lake

So when they arrived at the farm, everyone had to hear about her driving escapades. Sophie was a good driver, but it had to be fast.

They bought a new car every year. It was the most powerful car on the market. Sometimes it was a convertible and sometimes it was a hard top. Aunt Sophie had so many speeding and parking tickets in Duluth, Uncle Ozzy said, "The city will be able to lower the tax base as long as Sophie keeps driving and paying parking and speeding tickets."

Aunt Sophie proved her driving skills to Dewey and his family one afternoon. They were supposed to come for supper on Saturday about six o'clock. They didn't come, so Dewey's family ate and went to milk the cows. It got to be about six-thirty and they heard a police siren in the distance.

Dad said, "It must be Frank chasing Sophie".

They all said, "Really?"

"No I was just kdding." said Dad.

Suddenly up the road in a heavy cloud of dust, a sports car came sliding sideways. It barely made it onto their driveway and almost slid into the ditch. Sophie gave it the gas, then slammed on the brakes, and slid to stop in front of the barn. Wow! Dewey had never seen such powerful driving. It had everyone all pumped up. The dust finally settled (all of the roads at that time were gravel). When it is dry a speeding car could kick up a lot of dust.

By the time Constable Frank (the local town police) pulled up with lights flashing and siren blaring, Aunt Sophie was leaning against the back fender.

Gosh, she looked beautiful, all decked out as usual. She was as calm as a butterfly. Maybe in her dreams she thought she was a movie star and life was just one big stage.

Frank knew her and she knew him. As he got out of his police car she said, "Well, hello there Sheriff."

Dad knew Frank very well. After all, it was a small town and every body knew every body. Everyone watching had a smirk on their faces and wondered what would happen now. Mom was terribly embarrassed for her sister.

So Frank said, "You were speeding through town Sophie!" He was mad.

Aunt Sophie loved to have an audience, so she played her heart out. She was Olivia de Havilland, Greta Garbo, the Gabor sisters, and Marilyn Monroe all rolled into one. It was wonderful. His aunt could have won an Oscar for her performance. She talked her way out of many tickets through the years but this had to be the best.

Frank left just giving her a warning. But she could not let him leave with the last word, no sir! Not Auntie Sophie!

As Frank got in his car, she said, "My car can beat your car."

That was a sore spot because it was true. Frank had the Ford Interceptor Series. She had the new Studebaker Sports Car. It was one of the most powerful cars on the market at that time.

Frank said, "Where is Ozzy? Is he working?"

Sophie answered, "No, we had an argument about who would drive and he said he didn't dare ride with me. That's why I am so late for supper with my sister and her family!"

They were a good fascinating family and when they each passed away, they were missed very much.

Dewey laughed to himself as he thought back to the Sophie days. Those were exciting times for their family.

- 8 -

4-H DAYS

When Dewey was nine years old, he joined 4-H. He joined the Happy Hour 4-H Club. It was the oldest club in the county. For the eleven years of club work that he experienced, he knew he had the best 4-H leader in the world.

She led the group of children; she did not do the work for them. Everyone did so much and learned so much from Mrs. Eckman.

Dewey started with gardening and a young Jersey calf. The whole object was to get his project ready for the Carlton County Fair. Everyone hoped for a blue ribbon on their project. But, all Dewey got that year was white ribbons for all his projects.

He even got a white on his conservation project which was his pride and joy. It was a book report about Smokey the Bear and his saying "Only YOU can prevent forest fires!" His projects just did not compare with everyone else.

The next year it was pretty much the same thing. For the garden project he had picked peas, beans, carrots, radishes, and onions. This was the second year of white ribbon on gardening.

His conservation project was not good enough – got a white ribbon. His Jersey calf which he picked, that he thought was the best one in the county, also got a white ribbon.

He had very high hopes for his third year because he worked so hard on everything. At last he got a red on his garden and another red on his calf. He always picked a different calf every year hoping it would do better.

Each year there was a 4-H event called the Northeast Dairy Days sponsored by the American Dairy Association. It was held in June, which was designated Dairy Month in Minnesota.

Every year a different town in northeast Minnesota was chosen to host Dairy Days. The dairy kids were always very hopeful that this year would be the year they were going to win.

Dairy Days was known as a very upscale 4-H dairy show. The judges were the best in the United States.

The champion animal from each breed had a picture taken by the best cattle photographer in America. As you can imagine, the animals had ideas of their own sometimes. Just to get the perfect pose with an animal might take up to two hours. The photographer never gave up until he got the picture just perfect.

So the kids and their animals got judged. Marylyn, a girl older than Dewey, was showing a nice Guernsey. She was always so smug - so haughty - so full of herself.

As the kids lined up before the judge with their animals, Dewey was right next to Marilyn. "Boy, I hope I beat her." he thought.

In the line up, there could be several animals that got blue, red or white ribbons. The judge started giving out the blue ribbons. Sure enough, Marilyn got a blue and she was told to come back for the showmanship competition.

Showmanship was the highest competition of all of the animal competitions in 4-H. This was where all the breeds showed against each other for the coveted showmanship trophy.

Since Dewey was standing next to Marilyn he thought for sure he would get a blue ribbon too. After all how could you not give a blue ribbon to a beautiful, brown eyed Jersey? They were the favorite in the barn. Everyone came to the barn to look at the animals with the large, soft, dreamy brown eyes. Nobody came to look at Guernsey cows. They weren't even pretty and besides they had pink eyes. They looked like they had a disease.

Dewey was ready to receive his first blue ribbon in his life. But to his dismay, the judge gave him a red ribbon and his heart sank. He wanted a blue ribbon; he felt that anything less than that was failure.

Dewey's disgust about the whole judging thing must have been showing. Marylyn said, "Why do you keep coming to these shows? You are never going to win anything with your junk. And you look as bad as your animal."

Dewey felt sick to be told that he was worthless, especially by a girl. His eyes were welling up with tears that he strained to hold back. He could not cry in public, especially not in front of Marilyn and have the whole world see what a failure he was! It was like the Hee-Haw Show song "Deep dark depression, excessive misery – Oooooooooooo!"

That was the lowest point in his 4-H career. He was ready to quit. He could not stand the humiliation. And he sure did not want to go to the County Fair in August. He was certain he would be humiliated for four days. At least Dairy Day was only one day.

In those days a kid could stay in 4-H until the age of twenty-one. Dewey was determined that he was quitting right now.

Someone talked Dewey into staying in 4-H. That someone was his club leader, Mrs. Eckman. Thank you, Mrs. Eckman.

Then something clicked in Dewey. That something was what makes people competitive. It was what makes people try harder to change. It was what helps you want to do it differently.

He started to learn from others. He saw what made them successful. He went to judging seminars put on by the County Extension Office. The County 4-H Extension Agents were very helpful. They taught him about what the judges look for.

This was a good start for him and he began to have hope. His eyes were opened and he could see how the others, like Marilyn, were able to get blue ribbons. He could look at his own projects and see what changes needed to be made.

The American Guernsey Cattle Club was the most prominent breed in Carlton County. There were more Guernsey cattle in the county than any other breed. So, it was only natural for a Jersey breeder to try to beat a Guernsey breeder at the shows.

Well, Dewey went to the County Fair and he got a red ribbon in all his projects of gardening, photography, conservation, and his prize Jersey calf. Doors were being opened for him to go to other seminars.

The Forestry Research Center had camps for kids. He learned about growing trees from seeds up to transplanting them into the woods. He learned about shrubs, yard trees, and trees for windbreaks. He learned all about diseases that trees could get.

He stayed in a cabin at the Forestry Research Center run by the University of Minnesota. They would have about two hundred 4-H kids at each of these seminars. It was a wonderful hands-on educational experience.

In the spring, Dewey participated in judging seminars that took place right on host farms. He had many of these sessions on his parents' Jersey farm. They tried to have sessions on each of the farms of different breeds such as Holstein and Guernsey.

One of the most helpful to Dewey was the Olsen family in Barnum. Mr. Olsen was a wonderful teacher. He was a judge of dairy cattle. He was asked to judge prestigious cattle shows around America. He had a big family and they were all very helpful and kind. They were one of the nicest farm families in the county (even if they did have Guernsey cows!).

Dewey was taught how to see the traits of a winning animal such as its body conformation. He learned how to lead for Showmanship, grooming, and keeping his eye on the judge.

From about the age of twelve on, his years in 4-H improved tremendously. The knowledge gained from the University, Extension Agents, and other professionals helped him on a new career of blue and champion ribbons.

When he was in the ninth grade his shop teacher said that they could make anything they wanted. So Dewey had plans for making down hill skis.

His teacher gave him no help at all. Instead, he told him every day that he would never finish them. That it was too hard. He would never be able to bend the skis.

Dewey's best friend Richard's Dad had some nice oak boards he gave him along with the confidence to do it.

Dewey cut, shaped, and put in the groove underneath. His teacher teased him in front of the whole class about the fact that he would have to bend the skis on the ends so they would not get caught in the snow. Oh how they laughed.

But this was Dewey's third year with that teacher. He knew what an abusive person he was. When he had his skis ready to bend, he took them home. The teacher said, "Well, it will make fancy firewood."

Dewey's family had a steam hot water boiler in the milk house for cleaning milk utensils. Between the milkings, he would steam the skis. He would gradually tighten the bending clamp that he had made at home.

In three days he had a well bent pair of skis. He brought them back to school for the finishing sanding. He put on some ski boot clamps he bought new. They looked really nice.

His classmates were impressed. The day they all got their grades Dewey was down graded for bringing them home to bend them even though there was no way to do it at school. He received a D for all the work he had done.

At the Carlton County Fair, kids were required to give a written report about how they made their project. Dewey wrote up the whole process the best he could.

Well, Dewey got a blue ribbon at the county fair and a real nice note from the judge on his project. That little encouragement gave him enough encouragement to keep going and not give up on 4-H.

As they say, the rest is history. Dewey showed numerous cattle at the county fairs and Dairy Days. He earned many championships at the county fair.

He earned six trips to the Minnesota State Fair where he won the Jersey breed championship with Sally, his prize heifer. He experienced having his picture in all the newspapers. He also had the opportunity of having his picture taken several times by that world renowned photographer of cattle.

Finally, with such hard work and determination he got to a point of mentoring the younger kids coming up. It was fun and highly rewarding. He even became friends with Marylyn and so many of his peers from all over the state. It was what made him want to take over the home farm some day.

P.S. Thank you Marilyn for all the hardship you gave me. Now it is appreciated.

- 9 -

TAKING ON THE FARM

When Dewey was about fourteen his Dad got sick with diabetes. He and his Mom ran the farm. His Dad was able to drive the tractor for baling and other light duty farm chores.

To make up for his physical limitations, Dewey's Dad began building an insurance business. He was doing a good job and people knew they could trust him. He had good sales.

To keep the farm running, Dewey would milk the cows, feed and clean the barn, and catch the bus at 8:15 for school each day. His Mom would clean all the milking utensils. His parents were both getting up in age. All the rest of the kids had left home. It was only the three of them left to run the farm.

After school the whole schedule was repeated again as soon as he got off the bus. By the time he got all of the farming chores done, there was very little, if any, time or energy left for doing school work. There was absolutely no time for sports or other extra curricular activities. It took a lot out of him.

Dewey had enjoyed farming all his life. But there just was not enough money in it. They made it with perseverance and prayer.

His school work suffered a lot as he kept the farm going. He did not have as much time to spend on it as most of his classmates.

Just like right now, his typing was not too much better than almost fifty years ago. His typing teacher in the tenth grade was good. He wanted his students to do well.

Mr. Lydeen, the typing teacher, was very hot tempered and would excuse himself from the room when he felt he could not control his hysterics. They were both entertaining and frightening.

Mr. Lydeen was dating Dewey's history teacher. She was a bit high strung also.

One day their personal lives jumped to the forefront of their school time. He was hollering down the hall at her things that should not be said in public. He was mad and that made her mad. So she started in.

This took place between classes when kids were trying to get to their next class. The hollering got pretty bad. Finally, Betty just slammed the door on her classroom to end it.

But that did not end it. No Siree! Mr. Lydeen ran down to her class and got his last word in. Or so he thought.

He stormed back into the typing room and told his students how stupid Betty was. He was so beet red that the school lunch could have been cooked on his head.

About two minutes went by. Suddenly, the typing room door flew open. Betty proceeded to inform him, "Don't you dare ever see me again."

Her head was also beet red as she slammed the door. Dewey guessed that she went back to her class.

By this time, Mr. Lydeen was livid. He was also embarrassed by all this. He just shook. He trembled!

He did have a reputation for throwing things and the students could tell he was desperate to throw something.

Electric typewriters had just been invented. The School had only purchased two because they were so expensive. That was all the School could afford. Because they were so valuable, like diamonds, only the special talented kids like Janet, were allowed to use them.

Dewey sat next to Janet trying desperately just to get his forty words a minute with three mistakes, maximum. Janet could type forty thousand words a minute while taking dictation, reading a book, talking on the phone, and eating lunch. Janet was amazing.

Oh no! It was going to be one of the great big electric typewriters which the School had just purchased. Janet's typewriter!

Mr. Lydeen picked up her brand new electric typewriter. Lifting it over his head, he smashed it in the middle of the floor at the front of the room.

Dewey wanted to ask if Mr. Lydeen would like to do his too. But he decided not to.

Mr. Lydeen came back a week later to apologize. He was allowed to finish the school year. However, neither he nor Betty came back the next school year.

Mr. Lydeen, wherever you are, Dewey has a bunch of computers and keyboards you can smash to smithereens. He is saving them for you.

Saturday afternoons, during the winter sometimes provided a little extra time for fun. Dewey and his friends would load up the truck with bags of feed for traction. Then they would take turns skiing behind the truck on the country roads. They would get up to thirty miles per hour. They needed extra weight for traction because sometimes the roads would get very icy.

They would have a fifty foot rope to hang onto. It was just like water skiing behind a boat. One time they had three ropes and three skiers behind the truck. They skied all the way to a real small rural town. When they got there neighborhood dogs came after the skiers. These dogs were huge. The sound of the dogs' bark made the boys know that if the dogs caught them, the dogs would kill 'em.

The boys went through the middle of the town screaming at the driver to go faster. The dogs were gaining on them. But the driver thought he HAD to go the speed limit through this little town. By this time, they had been skiing for so many miles, they were just dead tired. Legs were just like jelly. They could hardly stand on their skis or hang onto the ropes. Every muscle throbbed with pain.

Finally, the dogs gave up! When the boys saw that, they just let go of the rope and fell to the ground and slid to a stop. They just laid there all sprawled out all over Main Street. The driver didn't even look back, he just kept going.

About the time they managed to get their strength back, the driver finally came back. They were all farm boys and had chores to do. That was the end of FUN for that day.

After this, the guys got together and decided they had to go faster than twenty or thirty miles an hour. So, they headed for the lake.

If the lake had six to eight inches of snow, it was perfect for skiing behind the truck. They would start at one edge of the lake and head for the other side.

Sometimes they would hook two ropes so two guys could ski at the same time. This was fun because they would criss-cross each other at about forty to fifty miles an hour just like the water skiers.

They always brought shovels with them. They would make piles of snow to make ski jumps. They were not big, but the skiers got two or three feet off the ground.

Sometimes both skiers would ski as far to one side of the truck as they possibly could. They were trying to put the truck into a slide. There would be a big cloud of snow thrown up when the truck went into a slide. The truck would slide in circles many times from the momentum. That way the driver got some thrills too.

One Saturday afternoon they decided to have a contest to see how fast they could go before the skier fell down.

Only one skier would go at a time because there was not enough traction to pull two for high speed skiing. He had to be able to get enough traction to get up to speed and also slow down when he got to the other side.

They found that the lake was not long enough. So they would start in approximately the middle of the lake and head for shore. By the time the driver got to shore he was going forty miles an hour. He would then make a big circle along the shoreline and head for the other side of the lake, gaining speed as quickly as possible.

Dewey was the only one of the skiers to go seventy miles an hour. He only did it once and not for very long because the driver had to slow down before sliding into shore. They needed a bigger lake!

One time Dewey fell going sixty miles an hour. It felt like he would never, ever stop rolling and sliding. His mouth, eyes, nose, and any nook and cranny between the clothes just kept filling up with snow.

One thing they worried about was fishermen who had fish houses on the lake. They would chop a big chunk of ice for a spearing hole. They put the ice outside their fish house. Then sometimes, they would move their fish houses to another place. No one would know that there was a block of ice on top of the snow. They would think about that when they were going seventy miles an hour, but not before.

When they got close to the other shore the driver would put the truck into a slide. The skier had the choice of passing the truck, falling down, or letting go and skiing into shore.

Sometimes on moonlit nights they would go out skiing on the country roads. The drifts were great for skiing. The problem with that was that they could not always see things like mailboxes, fence posts, fence wire, and drive ways that dropped off six feet. They would be going along when there was a sudden drop and just as quickly they were going back up again. Sometimes as they were going along the rope would hit a mailbox. What a rude awakening that was! They were soon cured of moonlight drives on country roads.

So, then they went back to the lake. They did a lot of lake driving at night. They did not do any high speed skiing at night because one of the skiers had hit one of those ice chunks. Luckily, he did not get hurt too bad, just a sprained ankle. It did start to make them think about the possibilities of getting hurt in the future. Thank goodness spring came, the ice melted, and they did not have to do that any more.

Dewey tried learning how to swim. But as he does, even to this day, he sank like a boat anchor to the bottom of any body of water. No matter how he tried to stay above water, he sank!

He was convinced that there were no lessons in the world, or flotation devices that could make him float. So, if you are ever in a boat with him, beware! It will probably sink.

His family can attest to this. Do not drown in his presence because he can't help you. They say everyone can float in the Dead Sea. He would like to try it some day. If he does, he thinks he will be dead in the Dead Sea!

His school years had their ups and downs, but for the most part they were good years. They were good training for life.

After graduation, he farmed for several years. He milked the cows and raised crops. Being on the farm, Dewey developed a real passion for farming. It was something he decided he wanted to do for life.

At this time the Vietnam War was escalating to the point of needing to draft older guys. So at the age of twenty-two, he got his marching orders.

This forced his father to sell their purebred Jersey herd that originated from the Isle of Jersey, just off the coast of England.

- 10 -

ARMY DAYS

As Dewey thought back, his service time for America seemed like it was just all a dream. So much had happened to this farm boy.

He remembered that the day before he left for Fort Leonard Wood in Missouri, he had been threshing oats. They threshed outs the old fashioned way with a twenty-two inch McCormick Deering separator.

The oats had been cut into bundles just two weeks before with a McCormick Deering binder. This tied the oats into bundles which were put into eight bundle shocks to dry. It made the field look like it was filled with tiny little teepees. He had to finish the job quickly because he was shipping out and there was no one else to finish the job.

The next day, his brother-in- law, Dick brought him down to the bus station in Moose Lake. At that time Dick gave him a serviceman's Bible. He also prayed a prayer for a safe journey.

The bus trip took him to the train station in Minneapolis and on to a place in Iowa where they picked up new recruits.

He made friends with a real nice Iowa recruit. This guy was about 6 ft 3 in. tall compared to the 5 ft. 8 in. tall frame of the kid from Minnesota.

The Army training was very rough. One of the first things everyone experienced was trying to survive without enough to eat and not enough rest.

The military was training them for the worst of combat. They were being trained in case they became prisoners of war in Vietnam. All the hard work on the farm had put him in excellent condition. However, a lot of guys did not have that advantage. These guys were wearing down already in the third week of training.

In barracks conversations, the guys all thought the starvation training was worthless. If they were captured, they would go through it for real in a prison compound and there would be nothing they could do about it. You do not really "prepare" for starving!

Their training began each morning with a two mile run with full combat gear. Those fall Missouri mornings were very cold but all the men wore were t-shirts and cotton fatigues.

The calisthenics before breakfast at 6:00 a.m. were next. The men had no more than five minutes to eat. The Drill Instructors were constantly hollering "Eat 'n git out! Eat 'n git out! If you can't eat it, stuff it in your pocket!"

From 6:30 a.m. until 10:00 a.m. the men experienced constant running and going through things like on the TV program *Survivor*. There were many types of obstacle courses.

At 10:00 a.m. there was a five minute water break. Dewey was so fortunate that his Mom had sent bags of pre-sweetened Kool-Aid in the mail. He would mix this with the water in the canteen. The Missouri water tasted terrible compared to the best well water in the world on the farm.

The same activities were repeated again until about 1:00 p.m. when they had dinner. The cooks would bring hot stew out to the training areas. The men would get a "plop" of stew on their tin trays to eat. It did not look good at all! But when a person is really hungry, anything will taste good. It had to be eaten so fast, it really did not matter what it tasted like.

The afternoon was spent marching until between 6:00 p.m. and 7:00 p.m. Then it was suppertime. Again, they had five minutes to eat.

Finally, the men could take a shower and "spit shine" their boots and get everything in order for the next day.

Everyone had to take a turn for two hour guard duty shifts. Each of the barracks had their own guard duty. Sometimes, they would just get to sleep and the Drill Instructors would storm the barracks. They would make up an emergency to see how the men would react.

One night it was a missing rifle cartridge. The whole barracks was turned upside down. All the foot lockers were dumped out. Then the Drill Instructors would get tired of the whole thing and leave. The men had to clean up the mess. By that time, it was morning and time to start the routine all over again.

One night the cartridge must have been out in the yard area of the barracks. So the men all had to go on their hands and knees looking through the grass for a rifle cartridge they knew was not there. But like the good soldiers they were, they did what they were told.

One night an ambulance was called to one of the barracks. His friend, Tom, had a very fast moving spinal meningitis. He died a very painful death.

About twelve other guys got sick at the same time. They were hospitalized for a long period of time. Three of the twelve barely survived. The harsh training had finally taken its toll. The men were so worn out; they were susceptible to just about everything.

Tom's family came to Fort Leonard Wood for the funeral. Tom had been in Echo Company and Dewey was in Delta Company. Out of five hundred troops from five companies, the military picked him to lead the procession carrying the American flag.

The military had no way of knowing that Tom had been his best friend, so it was amazing that he had been picked for such an honor. Even though he lost his friend, carrying the flag and leading five hundred men who, by that time, were really an impressive marching unit was nearly overwhelming.

He could feel the muscles and tendons in his legs stiffening to the point that it was difficult to put one foot in front of the other. All of the troops were feeling this drain in their bodies and they all realized that the next one to go to the hospital and not return could be them.

When they passed his friend's mourning family, he felt so sad for them. They had lost a really good son and he had never even been in a battle yet.

Another amazing thing was that the day of the funeral, the men had the day off. They had time to do what needed to be done. They even had a chance to eat good meals and plenty of time to eat it.

Shortly after the funeral, there was an investigation into the training methods. The Drill Instructors had been to Vietnam. They had experienced first hand what the troops were going to face. They were so impassioned about preparing them for what they would go through, that they went overboard in their training strategies.

One of the returning combat soldiers was brought in to speak to all of the five company troops.

He said, "You better learn everything they teach you or you're going to die out there!"

He wanted the men to know they better take the training seriously. It was not a joke. He was so determined that the men learn how to protect themselves that he ended up screaming and loosing control. It must have been battle fatigue.

The Commander and the Drill Instructors thought they were doing the right things to prepare the men, but they went too far. The Commander of the unit was relieved of his position because everybody was getting sick from not getting enough to eat and not getting enough rest and sleep.

After they got a new Commander, things got a lot better. They had the same Drill Instructors and they agreed that they had gone too far and caused all the hardships. The men were given more to eat and even a little more rest.

After eight weeks of basic training, Dewey had another eight weeks of Advanced Individual Training. All of his tests indicated that he should be a truck driver.

The Army assembled all the men who tested with similar abilities from around the entire United States. They started training them to drive jeeps, three quarter tons vehicles, and deuce 'n half trucks. Dewey enjoyed it. He had always loved driving.

First he was required to participate in intense training on the inch and a half thick Army driver training manual. All this was done in a large tent out on the vehicle driving range. The tent was dark and even though it was cold outside, it became very warm in the tent. This made the men sleepy.

Part of the training included watching movies. During these movies, the Drill. Instructors would come around with a flash light to see if anyone was sleeping during the film. If they were caught sleeping, they had to drop for fifty push-ups.

Next there were the written tests. They took eight grueling hours. He did very well on this test.

With all the book learning completed, it was time to get in the vehicles and learn how to drive them. This was fun!

He enjoyed this part immensely. He could drive a stick shift of any kind. Driving the obstacle course was great, especially with the jeep.

There was a really steep, long hill. He had to go in a convoy. Everyone had to stop and take it out of gear. Then they had to start all over again to go forward without rolling backwards. Some guys killed the engine. Some of them could not pop the clutch fast enough and they rolled back. This was so funny. It had a real domino effect. One slammed into the vehicle behind him, which caused that one to do the same. It just repeated itself all the way down the line.

Another funny experience was night driving with the lights turned off. They had to drive the same obstacle course. This time it was so dark and foggy guys kept banging into the jeep in front of them. Sometimes they would get up to thirty or forty miles an hour. The guy in front would slow down because he couldn't see. The one behind him would slam into him because the one in front had no brake lights. Thank goodness these jeeps were made with good bumpers. There were no seatbelts so they were jostled around a lot.

Finally, they got to take the two-day behind the wheel and oral driving exam. The test was taken using all the different kinds of vehicles. In the deuce 'n half, he had to back up to a dock without using the mirrors or looking back. He had one chance to stop and he had to be within two feet of the dock. If he wasn't, he would fail that part of the test.

When he came to this part of the test, he drove past the dock so he saw where it was. Then, he drove right up to where the Drill Instructor was standing. He turned the mirrors down so they could not be used. As he backed towards the dock, the Drill Instructor walked next to the vehicle just ahead of it, always reminding him to look straight ahead. Dewey backed up fast. He watched the Drill Instructor's facial expression to know when he would hit the dock. Suddenly, he slammed on the brakes. The Drill Instructor measured the distance. He was eight inches from the dock!

He could never figure out what the point of that was. Why not **LOOK** where you are going?

Everyone should have to go through at least part of what they went through. It really made one think about driving.

Dewey graduated eighth in a class of two hundred and fifty drivers. Everyone was trained for combat, so they all figured they were all going to Vietnam.

He had been given a wish list of three choices of places to serve. He put Vietnam as his first choice. Next he thought Germany would be good. His third choice was Alaska. In the sixteen weeks of total training, they were all given the three top choice papers three times. He filled it out the same every time.

Well, the training was done and they were now considered lean, mean, fighting machines. Then they were sent home for Christmas vacation.

When he was home, he got his orders. He was being sent to the polar training camp at Fort Wainwright up in Fairbanks, Alaska.

He got to St. Louis, Missouri just fine. But then he discovered that he had missed the old troop plane for Chicago. This was not good! He wondered how in the world a country boy like him would ever figure out how to get to Chicago and what was it going to cost him.

With the help of a very nice airline company, they had a seat open on a flight to Chicago. They held it for him. He ran the long, long, long hallway to where the stewardess was waiting for him. They really took good care of him. They gave him a great breakfast. It was a comfortable flight.

He got to O'Hare Airport a half an hour before the other guys. And it only cost him ten dollars.

Then it was on to Fort Lewis in Seattle where it was 70 degrees. That was quite a change for a fellow from Northern

When Satan Came to Moose Lake

Minnesota where it was winter. They were there for three days getting the paper work done. It was considered overseas duty as well as hazardous duty. So there was extra paper work. This also meant extra pay for the Alaska troops.

Next, they flew on to Fairbanks, Alaska. He disembarked the plane to discover that the temperature in Fairbanks was forty degrees below zero. That was a drop of one hundred and ten degrees from Seattle.

Of the two hundred and fifty drivers, eight of the men were sent to Alaska, two were sent to Korea and twelve were sent to Germany. All of the rest went to "Nam...."

Their first job when they arrived in Fairbanks was to get warm, polar clothes. They proved later not to work very well when he had to drive. Staying warm and driving were not going to always happen at the same time.

Dewey discovered that they now had to take the written Alaska driver test. One would have thought that a Minnesota driver's license and the training he had at Fort Leonard Wood would have been sufficient, but not so.

Then the men were brought into the motor pool. Here the First Sergeant asked if anyone had driven a bus. Of course not, they had been trained to be truck drivers.

The First Sergeant then asked if any one had ever ridden a bus. Naturally, all of them had done this. He then said, "Okay, you are now bus drivers."

"Anderson, you are first to take a behind the wheel test." he said.

Having his name start with "A" always meant he had to do things first. They did everything alphabetically in the Army.

So they all went out to the parking lot. About ten officers and NCO-s got on the bus. By the way, NCO means Non-Commissioned Officers, such as sergeants.

When Satan Came to Moose Lake

One of them said, "Okay, show us how you drive." Dewey found first gear and took off. Then he found second and went forward some more.

Someone said, "Stop. Back up." So he backed up.

"Stop. Open the door."

When he stopped the bus, they all started getting out. He asked them, "What did I do wrong?"

They laughed and said, "Nothing, you are an official Alaska driver now. We only wanted to see if you could go forward and back!" Wow! That was some test!

They had ten drivers to do the job of twenty-five drivers. They were assigned their own bus. It was a forty-five passenger Detroit diesel pusher.

He loved his bus. During his time in Alaska, he put on one hundred and seventy five thousand miles. He accumulated all these miles driving shuttle routes, school kids, troops, extra curricular trips all over Northern Alaska, two airport runs seven days a week, and many other trips. There were very few cars on post so everyone depended on bus service.

The drivers kept their buses running twenty-four hours a day in the winter. Each bus had a one hundred gallon fuel tank. It was so cold all the time that when they drove a straight stretch, they had to stop the bus and try turning the steering wheel back and forth. That was because the power steering oil would freeze up. They also had to constantly try the air brakes to be sure they were working.

Dewey was on very tight schedules. He drove eighteen hours a day, seven days a week, for six months before he got a day off. This was at the height of the Vietnam War, which made great shortages of personnel at a lot of the bases.

The cold brought many other problems. The high school had seventy girls get pregnant. The suicide rate was very high. This was supposedly because of having almost twenty-four hours of darkness everyday during the winter.

Sometimes during those long, dark winter days and nights, the guys would figure out a prank to pull on someone. At seven o'clock one evening, one of the divers who had driven all day came in. He was too tired to eat. He just laid down on his cot and fell asleep. The guys let him sleep an hour and then woke him up.

"Pack! Aren't you supposed to do that "Tack One" run at eight this morning?"

Oh boy! He jumped up and took off for the motor pool three blocks away. Two hours later he came back. He was mad. He was fit to be tied. It was still night time, not morning! But how can you tell when its dark twenty-four hours a day.

The guys never liked Pack very much. He was a sarcastic person who would lie and go behind people's backs to the Sergeants to try to get his own way. Dewey always thought Pack would have fit in good with Moose Lake with the kind of meanness he showed others. That saying "What goes around comes around" usually come true. If you are mean to others, it eventually comes back to you.

By the way, Tack One was a radar missile site. There were hundreds of these sites in Alaska during the "Cold War". Russia was only a short distance from Alaska. During the winter, when the ocean was frozen people could actually walk across from Russia to Alaska. The United States needed to be protected in case Russia decided to attack. They were constantly being trained to be on guard for subversive activities.

The first winter he experienced winter driving in Alaska. One of the hardest driving experiences was finding his way through the ice fog. He had never seen ice fog before. It was so cold for such a long period that the moisture in the air would freeze and make ice crystals that stayed in the air. All the Army busses were equipped with fog lights. Regular lights just reflected back and he could not see anything.

When he did his school bus route on the post, he had to really concentrate so he would not get disoriented. He had to count the streets to keep track of where he was.

Ice fog lasted for many weeks. With twenty-four hours a day of darkness, it was just as cold in the bus as out. The diesel engine just could not put out any heat.

Remember the warning? **"Don't put your tongue on the pump handle?"** Well, Dewey had his load of kids and was heading for the school. A bunch of kids were all excited and anxious for Melody, a second grader half way back. She got her tongue stuck to the window.

The more she squirmed to try to get loose, the more of her tongue got stuck. The bus had no CBs or radios of any kind for communication. He would have to help her as best he could. That's the way it was forty years ago.

When he finally was able to get back there, her face and nose were flat against the window. Her tongue was extended as far as it would go. He was so amazed at how calm she was. No one else was!

Dewey told Melody that he was going to go outside and put his hands on the window to thaw it out. He hoped that the heat from his hands would warm up the window enough for her to get loose. It did not work because his hands were too cold to do any good.

Then one of the "helpful" high school boys said to just pull her off. Boy that would have probably torn her tongue right out of her mouth.

Dewey had to get the rest of the bus load settled down before he could do any thing for Melody. Then, he put his right hand on the back of her head to hold it still and stable. He got his face against her face and started blowing his hot air around the window. Then he soaked his fingers in his mouth and slobbered hot spit around her tongue, nose, and cheek. It took a long time, but finally it started to thaw faster than it froze.

When she was almost free she was going to yank the last tip of her tongue but Dewey held her tongue and thawed the window to free her tongue. The tip of her tongue was frozen solid for about a half inch.

She had a hard time to even get her tongue back in her mouth it was so swollen. Dewey told her to be very careful. He told her that he was going to bring everybody to the school.

When they got to school, he told the students to get Melody's teacher. He went back to check on her. She was crying and scared. He put his arm around Melody. He brought her close to breath warm air. When a person thaws out from freezing their skin feels like it is on fire. She was scared of her tongue being stretched for life. Being a Minnesota boy, he could assure her that she would heal up okay.

Her teacher heard what happened and came out to the bus to get Melody, who was pretty weakened by her trauma.

Dewey had many routes to pick up for several schools, so he had to leave right away. Taking care of Melody had put him way behind schedule. You could not leave kids waiting at the bus stop for very many minutes because they would freeze or get frost bite.

Melody did heal up and her tongue did shrink. From that time on, every time she got on his bus, he got a big hug. She stuck her tongue out at him as if to say, "See, I still got it."

He would tease her and ask her if her tongue fit in her mouth yet. She would laugh and wiggle her tongue in and out of her mouth. Each time she got on the bus, Melody would give him a big kiss on the cheek. And he would say, "Where's your tongue, Melody? Keep it off the window today!"

The hugs he got from all those Army kids were very rewarding. He loved them as his own. Sometimes they would slip and call him, Dad. He got a kick out of that.

The kids came to know their bus driver as someone they could trust. So everyday there would be students who would ask for help with math or history or even personal problems.

Dewey was also the designated driver for the United States Army marching band. The band had the tallest person he had ever seen in his life. This guy was six feet ten inches tall. He set the cadence and carried a very large, ornate baton as they marched and played in all the parades. They gave concerts when dignitaries came to Fairbanks. It was a great honor to be chosen to drive for them.

Dewey spent 1967 and 1968 up in Alaska. While there he was the designated driver for the I.G. team. I.G. stands for Inspector General. They traveled the world inspecting Army posts. They were good. One of their many orders from Washington was to try infiltrating a missile site.

He hauled them half way up the mountain and let them off in the woods. He was given no explanation except for his orders to meet them in that same spot in three days. He was told to keep it all top secret.

When it was time to pick them up, they were in a real big hurry to get out of there. They were running away from the missile site guards who were supposedly chasing them. Dewey could hear the guard dogs in the background. They were getting closer. He needed to get these men out of there right away.

The ranking officer was a Lieutenant Colonel. Ten of his men were trained in subversive activities. This was very dangerous work. After they got down the road several miles, they started to relax. The adrenaline rush faded away and they laughed. They laughed so hard because they had won. They had accomplished their mission.

When the Blue Angels came to put on their precision flying performance, he brought them from their jet planes to their quarters. They were good natured guys. They kidded him about how far off the ground his rig could go.

Dewey said, "You just don't want to know!"

Dewey had worked his eighteen hour shift and gone to bed about eight o'clock in the morning. He was sleeping in his bunk when about nine in the morning, he was suddenly awakened by a big chunk of plaster ceiling that dropped on his chest. It was a three foot by one inch thick piece of plaster. The whole building was vibrating.

He had absolutely no idea what was going on. He got up and looked out the second story window of his barracks. People were running all over the place. That was when he saw the Blue Angel pilots running for their jets. They were off and in the air in minutes.

The earthquake was the worst in Fairbanks' history. The post hospital ended up having a big crack right down the middle, from the top down to the big entry doors. About the only buildings that did not get damaged were log houses that just sort of rolled with the waves.

If you were in a boat on a calm lake and suddenly you were overtaken by numerous waves; that was what Dewey thought an earthquake felt like. It was like suddenly being thrust in the middle of a war zone. Buildings were tumbling everywhere. People were running and screaming. It was scary to say the least.

Normally, Alaska is a beautiful state. Dewey had the best job in the world. But no matter where a person is, sometimes the worst conditions can be experienced. Thankfully things like this do not happen routinely.

Imagine, way up there in tundra country they have hot water springs coming out of the ground. One of the places was Chena Hot Springs, located about fifty miles north of Fairbanks. They made a real nice resort with a big swimming pool.

To the west of there, about one hundred and fifty miles, there was one called Manley Hot Springs. The people who owned Manley put a greenhouse type of building up. They built four cement tanks that were eight feet square.

The hot water from the mountain side was diverted from one tank to the other. You could pick the heat you wanted. The first one was just too hot for him, so he tried one of the other tanks. You could actually only use two of these tanks because the first two were just so hot.

These people also grew lots of exotic flowers. Grape vines covered the steel roof trusses from one end of the building to the other. The building was about twenty-four feet wide by sixty feet long.

He could relax in the tanks and reach up and eat grapes. You would not believe that way up in Northern Alaska the gigantic grapes on those vines! Five grapes would make a meal. This was one of the many fun times he experienced while in Alaska.

Summer of 1968 came and brought with it the worst flood in Fairbanks' history. It had rained so much up where the Chena River began in the mountain regions that the water over flowed its banks and flooded Fort Wainwright and Fairbanks.

The air strip on base split the Fort. The river flowed around the end of the air strip and then went through Fairbanks.

The flood was a surprise to everybody. It came so fast that they did not realize that it would be a major catastrophe. From the second story of the barracks, the men watched the water rising. Manhole covers pushed up and out of the way as water gushed up from the storm sewers. The water started flooding across the main road. The river, with its swift current, started rising fast. The men knew this was really going to be a terrible, dangerous situation.

The men were told to get the motor pool vehicles to high ground. They had to go at least a half a mile from the motor pool side of the base across the runway to a higher mound of ground that was thought to be safe.

The first convoy of eighty vehicles went across safely. It only took a half an hour. The men jumped into two busses to go back for more vehicles.

By this time there was a car almost totally submerged in the water. There was a mom and dad in the front seat. The two kids were in the back window deck waiting for help. A deuce 'n half crew was waiting on the side of the road to rescue them.

The raging waters of the Chena River had made it impossible to use the road, so they had to go across the airstrip. In two hours time, the Chena had covered the whole fort and was flooding Fairbanks.

For the second convoy Dewey was designated to drive the military police van with red flashing lights to signify that he was the last vehicle. About one quarter of the way across, suddenly the heavy current took his vehicle to the edge of the ditch. It was eight o'clock at night and pitch dark.

The water was up to his neck in the Ford Econoline van. Of course, the engine was stalled. His frantic calls on the police scanner failed because the communication center had been abandoned.

His van was teetering to the side ready to tip over and roll into twelve feet of water. It would not take much to tip it. Only one head light showed up over the water but the red flashing lights on top of the vehicle did get the attention of one person.

As he sat there awaiting his fate, he could see great big trees sailing down the airstrip river. One of those trees could wipe him out in seconds. Trees with great big roots that would span fourteen feet came just inches from his vehicle. There was one tree that had to be at least one hundred feet long.

Dewey was clinging to life. He never knew much about praying or what to pray. But this was a foxhole situation. His future life did not look good. He did not know GOD very well but he was praying fast for a miracle.

He thought he would never survive. It seemed like he had been in the waters for hours. He was about to give up, when he saw, way across the river, flashing lights.

He thought it must be a wrecker. He was hoping it was a wrecker. It was getting closer. It was backing up towards him. What a feeling of hope! This must be a miracle from God and it was definitely an answer to prayer.

It was his friend, Chief! He was their wrecker driver. He backed his wrecker, with three helpers hanging on the back, a quarter of a mile all the way across the airstrip through the raging waters of the Chena. God was with him too.

The wrecker crew hung onto the wrecker and wrapped the cable around the bumper of the van. Away they went.

The wrecker was a big heavy vehicle and stayed on the ground in spite of the current. However, Dewey's van was so light that the current took it sideways all the way to shore even with a full load of water. That was how swift and strong the current was.

After he was rescued, he got dry clothes from the supply depot. That building was built up high so the water never got into it. It only got as high as the loading dock which was four feet high.

He and another fellow took inventory of what they had. They were down to only two buses that would run on post. It got pretty exciting then.

The communication from Fairbanks hospital indicated they needed to evacuate immediately. They put all their flashing lights on and now they were emergency vehicles. They headed to Fairbanks to help with the evacuation of the patients and staff.

Their buses were so big and heavy they could go anywhere. The hospital was located just across the bridge on the banks of the Chena River. All night they worked with city bus drivers to evacuate people to the University of Alaska. The University was a few miles away up on higher ground.

There were a lot of vehicles lost in the flood. The next day, he could see cars actually floating on the river. He saw a semi truck in the water. All you could see was the top of the smoke stack.

The water stayed for two weeks before it went down. During that time, the two drivers worked around the clock. They slept in their buses. They picked up doctors to get them to hurting people from all over the area.

Dewey picked up a pregnant woman that waved him down. She was waist deep in water. He did not realize she was giving birth until he got her seated.

Now he was really scared. "It's coming! Help me!" she screamed.

He had delivered lots of calves on the farm but "Wow a woman? Deliver a real human baby!"

When everything was covered with water, it was sometimes hard to know exactly where the curb was, especially on a curvy road! There was a little bump in the road – Ouch!

He was not going to park at the curb and make her walk through two feet of water to get to the hospital. Blowing the air horn, he drove her right up to the entry steps of Bassett Hospital. Yes, over the curb, but a little gentler this time.

He laid on the air horn the whole way to the hospital and staff all knew something was up. Air horns could wake the dead, they were so loud.

Somehow, he had managed to get her there in one piece. He was kept too busy with all the rescues to ever find out how the pregnant girl or any of the others turned out.

Dewey thanked GOD for saving his life and he has forever been grateful. He also thanked Chief and his crew. Chief was an Indian from the Bemidji Red Lake area of Minnesota.

Dewey was out in the brigade area on an emergency run to pick up a doctor for an emergency at the hospital. There was only an inch of water on the road up there where he was located.

They got behind a long convoy of armored personnel carriers that was traveling very slowly. Since there was no traffic in the oncoming lane, with all his flashing lights on, he poured on the coals and took off around the convoy. He was doing about forty miles an hour.

Suddenly, the doctor asked him if he saw the wave of water he was making. The wave his bus was making was really a good one. It was at least twelve feet high.

He said to the doctor, "Do you see what is ahead?" The doctor started laughing and giggling like a kid. The lead vehicle had the Brigade Commander in dress blues standing up on top of the vehicle. He looked like General George Patton.

When they got along side him, he looked more like a generally drowned rat. The doctor was excited.

Dewey asked, "Well, do you think we should stop and see how the General is doing?"

They both laughed as he poured the coals on to get out of there quick. The doctor told Dewey it was the best ride he ever had.

Amazingly, there were no lives lost in this flood. But it had sure been close for Dewey and many other people.

Then the United States Congress sent a delegation to look over the damage. Dewey was the driver for them for the two days they were there. He hauled Vice-President Hubert Humphrey, some high ranking senators and congressmen, and a three star general.

There were millions of dollars in damages to Fort Wainwright. General Jones was relieved of his position for not taking the Army Corps of Engineer's warning to start sand bagging and preparing for a flood. The problem was that HE was in the bag. He was a nice man, but he had a big drinking problem.

Summer in Fairbanks was mild. There was twenty-four hours of sun light. The mosquitoes were so big they could carry a person away.

On the 4th of July weekend, Dewey had a load of troops he had to take down to Valdez for some R & R. It was a long trip but very beautiful.

The town of Valdez had been wiped out by the great Anchorage earthquake and tsunami that followed. In the early '60s they moved the town about two miles from the original sight.

To celebrate the holiday, the people of Valdez had a 4th of July pie eating contest for kids. The pies were made from native blueberries. Alaskan blueberries are pretty sour. The cooks did not put any sugar in those pies. A person had to be pretty tough to eat them.

Saturday night Dewey and one of his army buddies, Lynn, decided to climb a mountain. They got half way up by ten o'clock p.m.

Suddenly, a very heavy fog settled in. They lost their way and got into some sheer rock. They pulled and pushed each other to make it up to the top of the mountain.

Dewey had brought some flowers to plant at the top. Even though it was thick snow up there, he still planted them.

It got tremendously cold up there. They were soaking wet. They waited for about a half an hour. The clouds opened up just enough for them to pick a good way down.

They got back down about eight o'clock a.m. It was just in time for breakfast. They quickly changed clothes and began to make the four hundred mile trip back to Fort Wainwright.

August of 1968, when he left Alaska, was the year oil was discovered on the North Slope at Prudhoe Bay. That was five hundred miles north of Fairbanks.

During his time in Alaska, Dewey made many trips to Fort Greeley, a polar training fort. This fort was located one hundred miles south of Fairbanks.

One of these trips involved taking the little league baseball champions of Fairbanks to Fort Greeley for the state championship tournament.

The coaches brought a picnic lunch to eat on the bus as they could not leave Fairbanks until after five o'clock p.m. This was when everyone got off work. They shared their meals with Dewey as he drove.

The kids stayed in the gymnasium over night and played basketball in bare feet most of the night. The next day, their feet were so sore the kids could hardly walk let alone play baseball.

But before the kids could play ball, the field had to dry out. It had rained very hard over night. The sun came out and everyone with a rake worked on the infield but it would not dry fast enough.

So they got one of the big helicopters to hover over the infield. It was the kind with two big engines. As it dried the field, it blew the sand away and made a terrible mess on the bleachers and dug outs. These had to be meticulously spiffed up for this great event.

They decided to try plan B. They poured diesel fuel on the infield. They tried to light it but they could not get it to burn.

Well, time to go to plan C. About a thousand gallons of MO gas was poured on the infield. MO gas is a very cheap form of Army gas. Then the MO gas was lit.

Well, it burned and burned. The first game had to be postponed for two hours until the fires burned out. Then the sand had to be raked out.

The team Dewey was driving did not win any prizes that day but the trip home smelled like riding in a diesel tank. When the kids walked and slid on the field, they got soaked with diesel fuel.

There was a lot of waste in the Army. At Thanksgiving for example, the cook threw about twenty-five big frozen whole turkeys in the dumpster. Dewey could see this when he was parked out back waiting for another bus run.

The turkeys were fully wrapped. The Army just needed freezer space for a new shipment of food. Dewey had several friends who lived off post. They were married and could use a little extra help. So they each got a turkey. That helped Dewey too because he got a lot of good home cooking.

Some of the very best home cooking came from Chuck and Susie, who were from Indiana. They were his very best friends. They took good care of that Minnesota boy.

Susie moved up to Alaska to be with her husband. She worked as a registered nurse at the city hospital. Chuck worked as a bus driver with Dewey until he was promoted to E-5 which gave him a real cushy job with the brass.

When August 1968 came, Dewey and Chuck got their discharge orders at the same time. They were given three days to get to Fort Lewis in Washington state.

They drove the Al-Can Highway together. At that time it was fifteen hundred miles of winding, dirt road. Then it was another five hundred miles of tar road.

At Seattle, they were given their freedom papers and away they went. Homeward bound! Chuck and Susie got home and resumed their careers. They soon welcomed a baby girl into their life. As Dewey reflected back on the past, he smiled because now Kimberly was going to marry her high school sweetheart, Dane.

When Dewey got home, everyone was at the Carlton County Fair. So that was where he went. He found out that the community was quite indifferent to United States veterans. It was just as the Army told them when they were released from active duty.

The protest against the war was felt by a lot of vets. Dewey got out at the time Hanoi Jane Fonda was talking against America and supporting the Communist nations.

Dewey remembered a Fairbanks parade in which he drove his bus. He hauled the Air Borne troops on his bus. Normally, they would have actually marched but because of the threats against the troops by fellow Americans, it was not advisable.

Sure enough, the people lining the streets of Fairbanks threw bottles and eggs at his bus. They ran up to spit on the bus. They hollered obscenities at our troops who were fighting to keep the freedoms of the United States.

It was a terrible tribute to some highly trained troops. They had put their lives on the line to protect those who think they have the right to protest that way.

People who treat our service men and women like this are traitors to America and should be treated as such. It is disrespectful to burn the American flag and people who believe they need to do this should go live in a communist country.

The place to protest was then and still is at the ballot box, and on the floor of congress, and in the newspaper.

People should take note of who is instigating these protests. It is mostly college professors who hate the foundations of America and insight young people to disrespect America and all that she stands for.

Nowadays, Hollywood is in the forefront of leading the disrespect for our troops who willingly put themselves in harms way each day so that individual Americans can have all of the freedoms that America offers.

- 11 -

LOOKING BACK AT MOOSE LAKE

Dewey thought back on his little town. Moose Lake started out just like any small, rural town. It met the needs of the local people and had potential for growth just like many other little towns.

But the fact remained, that Moose Lake had never ever grown the way it should have grown. In fact, it had shrunk.

The town leaders did not like this fact. They had always looked at Moose Lake as if it were the hub of the rural area. Many times people of Moose Lake acted as if they were superior to the people of the neighboring towns.

More recently, the town leaders realized it was not impressive to have the population dropping, so they got the state to add the state prison inmates at Moose Lake Correctional Institution as a population growth. So the town population doubled over night when the legislature gave approval for the prisoners to be counted as part of the town population.

These residents were the worst of the worst. They were rapists, molesters, and murderers. Three rows of razor fence surround the prison to keep the prisoners in and protect the townspeople from what these people could do to them. But that was what was going on at the present time, not what Dewey found when he returned from the army.

The prison used to be a state hospital for mentally ill people. The doctors that the state hired were doctors that graduated at the bottom of their class. They could not get a job in private practice. They were basically licensed drug pushers. That took place from 1950 through 1980.

The Moose Lake State Hospital had a big dairy farm. It provided all the milk, cheese, butter, ice cream, and meat for the two thousand residents.

The best part was that the higher level residents did most of the work. They milked the cows and made the hay. They also had sheep, pigs, and chickens.

Even some of the lower functioning residents could collect eggs. The pride these people had in the simple tasks they accomplished was priceless. They were so happy in their own little worlds.

There were also the apple and plum orchards and the vegetable gardens. The orchard provided lots of pruning, harvesting, processing, and eating.

The vegetable gardens had absolutely no weeds because weeds were not allowed by these hard working, proud residents of the Moose Lake State Hospital.

When people drove by the green houses containing flowers and other plants, the aroma of roses and lilacs and hundreds of species of plant life made them want to stay the night in the parking lot. A walk slowly around the beautifully landscaped lawns, with little gardens here and there, provided a breathtaking and relaxing experience.

He remembered back to the happy days in Moose Lake. They had just finished World War II. The war weary veterans came back to Moose Lake to start life anew, raise a family and work.

Many farms were built; many people were employed at the Moose Lake State Hospital. Other people built stores and services in Moose Lake.

The John Deere Store and Ellefson Farmall Dealership were two of the new farm stores. Several gas stations, cafes, grocery stores, a shoe store, clothing stores, and a dry cleaning service were created. Moose Lake became a hub for the whole area.

At the turn of the twentieth century, his Grandfather had the livery stable in the village limits. It was called The Pine Grove Farm. His "grampa" kept other peoples' horses overnight and fed them. He fixed wagons, greased axles, and shoed horses. It was kind of like a service station for horses and wagons.

Moose Lake had a good, honest school system. It had dedicated board members making decisions to educate students in the very best way possible. Just about everyone in the community was involved in the school in some way.

There was a high level of sportsmanship in football, basketball, hockey, track, and baseball. Every kid with passing grades was given a chance to participate.

Was everything perfect with the School? No! But back then issues were addressed and taken care of. If kids were wrong in their decisions, the consequences were given and they had quality time in the Principal's office to prepare their repentance speech and apologies for mistakes in their bad behavior choices.

In the first half of the 20th century in America, people did not worry about being politically correct. JUST DO WHAT IS RIGHT AND HONEST IN THE EYES OF GOD AND MAN. How simple. There were no drug problems. Sometimes kids would get some booze for Saturday night, but nothing was rampant.

Dewey thought back to when he was much younger. His Dad had great hopes for Moose Lake. Since he had learned this from his Dad, he shared that hope.

One day, his Dad got three neighbors together at his kitchen table. Back in those days local banks would not lend money to farmers. They thought farmers were too much of a risk. If there was a drought, there would be no crop and the farmer could not make the payment to the bank. If the barn burned and the cattle died, there would again be no payment to the bank. When the hail, the grasshoppers and locusts came, or there was a terribly hard winter, there would be no payment to the bank. Sometimes, if the husband died, the family was not able to carry on with the farm. Local bankers saw farmers as a risk and they did not want to involve the bank with them.

After much talk about these problems, they decided that they would start a credit union. His Dad laid five dollars on the table. He said, "Let's just start it right now. It will be called The Co-op Credit Union."

The Co-op Credit Union struggled in its first years. People put what money they had in passbook savings. These collected a little bit of interest. Then this money was lent out to farmers for their needed expenses.

In over fifty years, the credit union had seen phenomenal growth. It was now called Lake State Federal Credit Union, which had grown to five more locations. His Dad's #1 passbook was still on display in the Moose Lake branch. Go take a look.

His Dad also had been on the Moose Lake Township board for over twenty years. He served mostly as the chairman. He was very active in civic and political affairs. His Dad was a friend to Vice-President, Hubert H. Humphrey and Secretary of Agriculture, Bob Berglund.

He was a leader in Minnesota Farmers' Union. He was a delegate from the area for agricultural affairs. He was a strong DFLer.

When he got into his insurance business, he had more time and contacts with political figures. He helped campaign for the agriculture issues that he and the DFL had in common. The focus was on saving the family farm. It was their perceived idea that government subsidies were the answer for the family farms. That was a nice idea on paper but it worked the opposite of what they hoped. Bigger farmers got a bigger share of the subsidies and smaller farmers just stayed small and could not compete.

The subsidies actually put most small farmers out of business. It did not help that most young people found it was easier to make more money in the big cities than to stay on the family farm and work.

Dewey continued his reminiscing about what coming home from the Army had been like as he walked back to the house. He would soon need to get started cutting the hay.

- 12 -

AFTER THE ARMY

Dewey had looked forward to getting out of the Army and getting home. However, it had not been like he expected. Instead of being able to relax and just enjoy life, he felt agitated inside.

During his time in the military, just about every minute of everyday he was rushing to do something. After being home for about a month, he felt driven to do something more. For now farm life was not fast paced enough.

He weighed his options. He could always get a job. But he could also use his G.I. benefits and get some education. So he looked into what was available.

St. Cloud Technical School seemed to hold the best package. They were known for an excellent welding program. A skill like this would give him more job opportunities and certainly be useful on the farm as well. On the farm, he had a welder in the shop. He liked to tinker and make things.

When he looked into the school and the community, he found that St. Cloud was a large enough city that he would have no trouble finding work to help pay for his school expenses that were not covered by the G.I. Bill. So he started filling out the registration forms for the school, looking for a job, and finding housing he would be able to afford.

He got himself registered for classes just in time for the starting of the fall quarter. The welding program was a one year program.

He went to the St. Cloud Bus lines. He told them about his driving experience in the military and explained that he was going to the Technical College. Because of his classes, he would only be able to drive in the afternoon and evening. That was fine with them and they hired him immediately.

Finding housing went well too. He found reasonable housing not too far from the school. Here he shared a basement apartment with another student. The family was very nice and treated him well.

Because of his experience hauling kids in the military, the Bus Lines figured he would be well suited to handle a difficult route. They gave him the most difficult routes with the most rowdy and undisciplined kids.

The job actually consisted of three separate routes. The first one started at Central High School. These students were dropped off in St. Cloud all along Highway 23.

When he finished the first route, he went to Cathedral Catholic School. This was only half a load. To fill the route, he went across town to the Middle School to pick up those kids. This was also a good route and did not take very long. They were all very good kids.

His last route was the really hard one. It began at the Junior High School in north St. Cloud. He had the biggest bus in the fleet. It was a ninety passenger bus. They filled that bus plumb full, with three kids to a seat.

The first few days went alright. This was the longest of the three routes. These kids had to be bussed all the way over to Waite Park.

They found out very quickly that Dewey was a military man and they gradually started to test him. He was a stern bus driver. He was not afraid to look them in the eye. He was not intimidated by them. The rule was that the bus did not move until they were settled in their seats.

It took a few days for the rabble-rousers to figure out how to handle their new bus driver. They had been through many bus drivers. No one else wanted that route anymore. They had developed quite a reputation for themselves.

They gradually became more and more defiant of his rules. At that time, one of the State rules for railroad tracks was that the bus had to stop before the tracks. One of the older kids was sent out to cross the tracks and look both ways to be sure it was safe for the bus to cross. Then he would wave or signal the driver that it was safe to cross. The driver picked the student up on the other side of the tracks.

At first it was not hard to get a kid to go out and flag the bus across. However, each kid that did this would get razzed so badly they refused to do it again.

One very outspoken boy, named Joey, was a tease. He tried to get Dewey mad at him. He was quick in thinking and had an answer for everything. He was really a smart kid. He was a real leader of the other kids.

One Thursday, no one would flag the bus. Dewey told them, "Fine, we'll just sit here until someone flags the bus." It was fairly light hearted. They were just going to see how far they could go with this new bus driver. So they sat there for a while.

Finally, Dewey said, "Hey, Joey, since you seem to know everything, why don't you go flag." Joey did not move.

So Dewey stood up and said, "What's the matter Joey? Don't you know how to flag the bus? How many of you other kids want Joey to go flag the bus?" The rest of the students were laughing and cheering Joey on.

"Go, Joey! Go, Joey."

Finally, Joey was going to show Dewey how to flag the bus. When he started for the door, Dewey said, "Now Joey, you know you have to look both ways down the tracks before you flag me across."

No eighth grader likes to be talked to as if they are a preschooler. The other kids loved this and laughed like crazy. Joey had never met his match before and the kids loved it.

Joey played up the part by saying, "I will help you get across the tracks." As he was heading down the steps, one of his quick witted ideas hit him in the head.

He turned to the kids and said, "Why don't you guys help me flag the bus across the track?"

Unbelievably to Dewey, all ninety kids left the bus. They just filed out the door. Joey was such a profound leader, the kids always did what he said. They never questioned anything. It was astonishing, to say the least.

As they went across the tracks, they looked back and danced and made all kinds of goofy motions. They said, "It's alright Mr. Bus Driver. You can cross the tracks now!"

Dewey laughed right with them. To his amazement, all ninety kids stood there and waved him across all ten of the tracks. Then when they got across the tracks, they all kept going, heading to their homes. They all just laughed and walked. It was a party. Some of those kids had two miles to walk home.

That was the shortest route he ever drove. He just went back to the bus garage. What else could you do with an empty bus?

He was the first one back to the bus terminal. The bus terminal owner was the only one there.

Dewey asked him, "Has there been any phone calls for me today?"

He answered, "No, Why?"

Dewey said "Oh, I was just wondering."

He went to get a quick bite to eat. Then he went to his other job at the Lincoln Avenue Garage. This was a welding shop. He worked here from six o'clock until midnight or one o'clock in the morning.

The welding shop made garbage dumpsters and industrial welding repairs, and many other projects. Dewey had various jobs at this shop. One of the projects he worked on was making the warning signs for highway construction jobs. He also made furnace heat exchangers.

One night the owner asked Dewey if he would like to go to Alaska to sell these heat exchangers for him. He knew that Dewey had been in the Army in Alaska. Being in school, he was not able to accept this offer.

Then he had school from six o'clock in the morning until noon. He grabbed a quick lunch. Then it was time for his bus route again at three o'clock.

At the bus terminal the next day, he asked if there were any phone calls for him.

"No, why?"

"Oh, I was just wondering."

Dewey did his other routes. Then he got to his bus load of middle school hikers. They all got on the bus so smugly. They felt like they had really pulled one over on him. They were good kids; it was just that none of the other drivers knew how to handle that age of kids. If you give them an inch, they will take a mile. This time some of them took two miles!

They all got seated. Dewey stood in front of them. Some were snickering. They had pulled the biggest prank on a bus driver in all their lives. But today was their bus driver's day! He had a plan. It was a risky plan, but those kids needed to learn a lesson.

He said, "I was thinking about yesterday and your walk from the railroad track. Were you tired when you got home? Some of you had a long, long walk. At least, it was a nice day for a walk. Some days are rainy, like today. When I got back to the bus terminal I had an extra half hour to kill. So I went down to McDonald's and had a nice big meal. I had a big hamburger, fries, and a strawberry shake. While I was enjoying sitting in an air conditioned McDonalds and eating, most of you were still walking home. I was thinking – why bring you all the way to the railroad tracks to walk home? If you got off here it would save me a lot more time. You would get a lot of exercise and fun. What do you think?"

He opened the door of the bus. He knew he was really going out on a limb with this one. "Joey, since you are a good leader and a good kid, why don't you come up here and lead them home?"

Then the kids started thinking. It got real quiet in the bus. Joey got more serious. Before he could come up with anything sarcastic, Dewey took one of the kids out of the front seat and put Joey in it.

When Joey got up there, Dewey got in his face and said, "Joey, you are going to be my flag man. We both know you know how to do it. From now on you're going to do it right. Do ya' hear me, Boy?"

Before Joey could say anything, Dewey addressed the bus load of kids in a very stern voice. "We all had our fun yesterday. But that was yesterday. Today and from now on if you pull a stunt like that again, I'll break every nose on your body! Do you understand me?"

Boy, did that make them think for the whole rest of the route. He never had a bit of trouble with those kids again for the rest of the year.

Dewey never told the bus company what a good bus route it was. There was never one complaint from a parent or the kids about anything for the remainder of the school year. He always wondered what ninety kids told their parents about walking home that one day.

At the end of that school year, Dewey graduated from welding school. He enjoyed welding school very much. He felt he had the best teacher in the world. His name was Bob Pratt. He had worked as a welder on the Alaska pipeline until his health was such that he could not take the coldness up there anymore.

After his graduation, it was time to go back to Moose Lake. He wondered what he would find this time.

- 13 -

STEEL PLANT DAYS

Just about as soon as he got back home, Dewey got a job working for United States Steel plant in Morgan Park, Minnesota. It was one of the oldest steel plants in the world. A lot of the steel making was antique and took a lot of manual labor.

When a person started working in those days, he started at the bottom of the work ladder. Boy was he at the bottom! He started as a cropper.

Giant red hot billets that were three feet by seven feet long were heated in huge, brick lined kilns. These were ten feet deep and about eight feet wide and sixteen feet long. The billets were in there for about two weeks. There were about twelve of these kilns. Each batch was a certain grade of steel such as high or low.

Sunday was a special day. Everyone at the plant knew that on that day they would be working with the steel for Caterpillar. That was the highest grade of steel made in the world.

The plant at Morgan Park was the only steel plant that could make this high grade of steel. That was because the atmospheric pressure had to be perfect. Being close to Lake Superior, the pressure and humidity worked together perfectly.

When the ingot was red hot and ready for processing, it was taken out of the kiln by a great, big overhead crane. It was put on a conveyor that brought the ingot to a big rolling machine. This machine squeezed the ingot back and forth until it became longer and thinner. It had to be done very fast before it cooled down.

When it got small enough, it was sent to another set of rollers that would continue making it even smaller. It finally ended up with four six by six inch ingots or six four by four inch ingots. It was then called a billet.

Then it had to be cut off so it would fit in a railroad car. The cut off man would cut both ends. The front ends had to be thrown off the conveyor very quickly. That was Dewey's job as a cropper.

With the six by six billets, there were four ends side by side. He used a pair of steel tongs to grab the ends. In order to do this, he had to stand straddling these hot billets as they flew between his legs. The front ends were about six to eight inches long. They were not so difficult to throw off the side into a recycling bin. But the back ends were as much as two feet long. These were much harder because they weighed so much.

It was so hot and heavy work that all anyone could work was twelve to fifteen minutes. He was then relieved by another cropper. He would actually work for fifteen minutes and be off fifteen minutes. This was repeated for an eight hour shift. The relief person had to be there immediately. The bosses watched everyone very closely for heat exhaustion.

Six of the four by four billets would come through at a time. They were much easier to handle. By the time the billets came to the cropper, they were between the red hot stage and the cooler black stage. Everyone had to work quickly, so the billets did not cool down too much before their job in the process was completed. If there was a hold up of any kind, the billet had to be thrown on the scrap iron pile.

Then the billets were sent to a cooling rack. As they came though, there was a man who would stamp each billet. He would hammer in the date and billet number. On the steel for Caterpillar, he added CAT. That was the only one that got a company name on the steel.

When it was totally cooled and cured, which took at least a week; it was loaded onto the railroad cars. The railroad cars came right into the cooling and curing part of the building.

Dewey had several promotions to different positions. He worked very hard. A person could apply for the various positions as they opened up. He wanted to get into the wire room. Before he could do that, he got into the rail plant.

The rail plant was a very dangerous place. That was where the lower grade billets were taken and rolled into rail size. They would then be used for fence posts, rerod and so forth.

Those red hot billets would be about two hundred feet long. At one point it came through the roller dye to a man called a catcher. It came through at about eighty miles an hour. He would have to catch the end of the billet with his tong. It had to be whipped around him and started into a smaller roller dye on the other side of him.

If it all went well, he had this red hot streaming steel rail flying around him in a small six foot area that he had to work in.

If he missed, the steel would shoot out into the rail plant area. Someone would sound an alarm, like a fire alarm. Everyone would run for their lives. The billet just went wild. As it went it cooled. They would end up with a two hundred foot piece of scrap iron dangling everywhere.

One time it chased Dewey and three other guys out a thirty foot door. It chased them right outside. Wherever they went, it went until it finally cooled down and stopped.

Then a fellow had to cut this billet into pieces using an acetylene torch. When it got cut, it could snap up and hit him in the head. The steel was under a great amount of tension and so were the men.

A year before Dewey started; a catcher had been killed by the rail when he was not paying attention. The two hundred foot, red hot rail went right through his stomach. There was nothing anyone could do. He died.

Dewey could not wait to get out of that department. Finally, he got a promotion to the wire department. It was clean. This was one of the higher paying positions at U.S. Steel. Besides his regular wages, he also received production pay for exceeding the shift quota. He always made over the quota.

In the wire mill, the cooled rails would go through a die. This machine brought it down to a roll of heavy half inch wire. Then the wire drawers would have to take the wire down to the size that was ordered. Each station was assigned a different size to make. They would be making barbed wire fence, stove pipe wire, or wire for nails. There was another department that made nails and staples.

Dewey enjoyed making wire. He would have four machines working at making different size wire at the same time. This was a good job.

The whole time that he worked at U.S. Steel there were rumors about the plant closing. Everyone was saying that this could happen at any time. They were encouraged to start looking for another job.

While working at the steel plant, Dewey was also working on the family farm. He had bought twenty-five Black Angus heifers.

When Satan Came to Moose Lake

On New Year's Day of 1971, there was a big snow storm. He had a date that afternoon to go snowmobiling with his girlfriend. Before he could go, he had to plow snow.

The snow was very heavy. It killed the engine of the small Farmall Super C tractor he was using. The battery was not charged up enough to start it back up. He went to crank the engine with a hand crank. He tried several cranks. With a stiff arm, he engaged the crank.

Suddenly the tractor started at full engine speed. It broke his arm jamming the two bones side by side in his fore arm.

The pain was excruciating. Dewey fell to the ground. He lay unconscious in the snow for quite a while.

When he came to, he could not see. He could only see outlines because everything was black. It was by instinct that he started crawling toward the house which was about one hundred yards away. He frequently blacked out on the way. It seemed to take him hours to get there.

Finally he got to the house. Simply by touch and feel, he got the doors open. There was one door for the porch and another door into the house. He slowly and painfully crawled up the steps to the kitchen.

The phone was on the wall. He was able to push himself up far enough to knock the receiver off the phone. It was almost as if he had gone blind. He could not make out the numbers.

The phone had a circle dial. By counting the holes, he was able to dial his parents' number. There was no "911" service in those days. His parents were living in town, so he was the only one on the farm. When they answered, all he was able to do was mumble the words, "Help me."

His parents rushed up to the farm. They found Dewey unconscious on the kitchen floor. They managed to get him up and out to the car so they could take him to the hospital.

Dr. Munster was on call. The nurses prepared Dewey for the surgery to set his broken arm. It was a really bad break and had done a lot of damage to the wrist and forearm. After three days, he was sent home.

Three months later, the doctor said his arm was finally healed. It was time to get the cast off. When the cast was removed, Dewey was surprised to find his arm and hand were not straight like before.

The forearm pointed downward about four inches before it got to the wrist. The doctor had set it crooked. It had a constant throbbing pain.

The doctor tried to convince him for about a month that there was nothing wrong with his arm. He said it was fine. Of course, it was not fine. Everyone who saw it could tell that it had been set wrong.

After this Dewey found out that the doctor, who set his arm, was a user of drugs. His own daughters also had free access to drugs. They were hooked really badly. He wondered how many other mistakes the doctor had made through the years because he was impaired.

Obviously, having his arm set wrong meant he would be handicapped for life if it was not fixed.

All of a sudden Dewey got a call from Dr. Munster telling him he had to be at the hospital immediately. Dewey was put into an operating room as fast as if it was a terrible emergency. As it turned out, the emergency was for the doctor.

Unbeknownst to Dewey, his Dad had contacted the insurance company and a lawyer. They had contacted Dr. Munster about this situation with Dewey's crooked arm.

To prevent a lawsuit, the doctor decided he better fix the problem before any lawyers got involved. He knew he could be charged with malpractice.

Dr. Munster had been a good doctor. He was a M.A.S.H. doctor in World War II. He had lots of experience as a surgeon. But when he began using drugs he started doing strange things.

About a year after Dewey's broken arm, the doctor was so high on drugs he took his pistol and started shooting up the neighborhood houses. He was hollering and staggering around. The police finally got him subdued.

After another eight weeks in a cast, the time came to take it off. Thankfully the arm had been set correctly. For many years he had pain in his wrist. There was also a strange lump on his forearm.

During the time that Dewey was healing up from his broken arm, United States Steel in Morgan Park closed down. Subsequently, Dewey had to find a new job.

- 14 -

A GROWING BLACK CLOUD

Well, he knew he would not get anything done by standing in his field thinking about the past so he headed for the house.

About half way to the house, there was a pond that he made some years ago. As he got closer to the pond, he glanced up. It seemed that the cloud over Moose Lake was really looking darker than usual today.

He had learned from the past that Satan was working on someone especially hard when the cloud looked like this. He hoped it was not someone he knew well that was going through difficult times. He also hoped and prayed that, whoever it was; they would have the strength to make the right choices.

It seemed that the "good people" of Moose Lake were not always strong of character and able to do the right thing. As for the town itself, there had been so many opportunities for good things to happen and then the whole thing would somehow just fall apart.

For years the City Counsel had felt threatened by anything new coming to town. The business men were terrified of competition. They even had a problem with taking care of the old Community Hospital situation.

Very few people ever heard about the big skullduggery the town fathers cooked up. You could say they got caught "with their pants down".

The City Council, which was separate from the Township, had a mayor. The Township had a chairman. The city fathers announced in the newspaper that perhaps a new hospital should be built. They thought it should be something more accessible. The old hospital had about twenty steps to go up to get inside. That would hurt a lot when a person's appendix was bursting.

Well, the Moose Lake City Council argued forever and could not agree on anything. Dewey believed it was the culmination of back stabbing, pervasive lies, and the fear that the elected officials had cultivated through the last thirty years that caused this problem. It was why Moose Lake has become one of the most distrustful places in America in which to live. Of course there are people here who will disagree but by now most of the honest thinking people have been run out of town.

For a small town there was an amazingly large amount of politics. There was world politics, national politics, state and county politics. And then there was Moose Lake politics. Sometimes they looked alike, but with less people involved small town politics should be up front and forth right.

In a small town where most everyone knows everyone else, one would expect politics to be more honest! In the old days you could count on just about everyone for help if it was needed.

How times had changed at Moose Lake. Granted many things that happen in politics are governed by the state and local government really had very little control. But that was not the situation in Moose Lake. Here it involved an attitude of selfishness and arrogance that lead to doing things behind closed doors.

In watching the workings of city and school proceedings over the last fifty years, he concluded that there was an extra amount of skullduggery in Moose Lake that he knew did not exist in other small towns.

Basically the population had been twelve hundred people for the last fifty years. The school enrollment had been right around the eight hundred pupil mark.

Even though the community really could use a new hospital, politics stood in the way and all that happened for the longest time was a lot of arguing and bickering.

Well, Dewey's Dad took up the matter with the rural farm organization. The consensus was that rural people saw a great need for a new hospital. So, they advertised the idea of a new hospital in the newspaper. They were going to have all townships in the area needing doctors, hospital services, plus an ambulance service involved in the process.

Until this time, the local hearse served as the ambulance. Imagine how it made an ailing person feel. To have the local hearse show up at his door did not exactly make him feel better. Many people chose to have a neighbor haul them to town in the back of a pickup.

The rural people worked very hard and got everything organized. It was time to put the ideas to a vote. The town and all townships voted to fund the hospital with property taxes and other funding available. The vote was a resounding yes except for one township, Split Rock.

Things moved along fast after the vote. The land was from the Moose Lake Township which was later annexed as part of the city. The architectural plans were approved. The water, sewer, and streets were put in. The building was built and ready for operation.

It was real ironic that the people of Split Rock refused to support the hospital and the very first ambulance call was to, you guessed it, Split Rock. That patient was one of the biggest foes of the project. After that episode, the Split Rock Township saw the need for the hospital and joined in support of the hospital district.

Apparently the City Council was a little miffed at how fast a bunch of dirt farmers could get things done. They showed their arrogance by their attitudes. Gradually, the newspaper articles made it sound as if it was the city counsel that got the hospital going and not the farmers. To this day, if you were to ask people how the hospital was started, the answer would be a resounding "Oh, the City of Moose Lake did that."

The Moose Lake Bank was always in the middle of all things going on in Moose Lake. They had a reputation for helping their close business friends but not the farming community. (Hence the building of the Credit Union mentioned earlier.)

The hospital was built in spite of all the crying of the city fathers. No one knew the number of secret meetings held by the city fathers and the Moose Lake Bank owners but they were caught with there pants down again!

You see, Dewey's Dad had begun a new career in the insurance business. He was one of the top salesmen in the state. The company he represented covered many public utilities insurance coverage.

His Dad heard on the street a comment from his competitor that insurance coverage bids would be opened the next evening. He did not tell the guy he was not invited to give a bid. So that evening his Dad got in touch with the state representative of his company and told him that he needed help quickly to get a bid in the next morning.

The expert was at their doorstep bright and early. The two of them worked all day and put together a policy which covered employees and the building, fire, wind, flood, and lawsuits. It included everything that could possibly be needed. This insurance company had policies with many hospitals throughout the nation. They knew exactly what coverage was needed. They had it ready for the seven o'clock meeting that night. They were both pumped up because it was a very good package.

They got to the meeting at exactly seven o'clock. His Dad told him later, "You could see embarrassment on the faces of these great and upstanding leaders of Moose Lake as they entered the room."

His partner did not notice at first and just introduced himself and started his presentation. It only took ten minutes. His Dad said it was impressive. But something was drastically wrong. It was dead quiet in that brand new meeting room of the Moose Lake Hospital.

There were only city people invited to the meeting. None of the rural people who had gotten the project going had been invited. These city people were too embarrassed to say anything. They just all sat there with droopy drawers.

Finally, the bank president spoke up and told Dewey's Dad and his associate that the meeting had been changed to six o'clock. They had just voted to give the bank the insurance coverage.

That was when the insurance representative, in a flash, put it altogether. It had all been a sham. The city leaders had gotten caught red handed. They refused to give local insurance companies an open bid for insurance coverage of the new hospital. The bank was going to "git it all".

They would be charged with violation of the open meeting laws. This was public government so there was also talk that some insurance fraud had taken place in the way it was handled.

The bank and the city were scared of the lawsuit which his Dad's associate was beginning to put into place. The bank made some concessions to his Dad. They were actually underhanded threats to call off the lawsuit and then all insurance agents in the hospital district would get a dividend for the premiums paid. His Dad was such an easy going guy; he talked his associate into backing off.

Some weeks later, one of the other insurance agents confided to Dewey's Dad that he knew nothing of the underhanded set up of the insurance scandal. He said the city fathers were mad because the rural people got the job done and they did not. The man also said that the insurance company his Dad represented gave coverage the bank never thought of, such as employee coverage.

The town fathers kept their distance from his Dad after that. But they were a minority of people from the town, like about ten people. The rest of the community knew nothing about it. They were happy to have a new hospital.

This hospital episode happened many years ago. Now as Dewey stood there remembering the history of Moose Lake, he realized that underhanded things like that never stopped happening in Moose Lake. He never would have dreamed that these underhanded antics would come as close to home for him as they did in 1998.

He now realized that the Moose Lake papers do not report the important news that the community really should know about. They demonstrated that by their participation in the great cover up by the Moose Lake Public School back around 1998 -99.

The State report on drug and alcoholism use by high school students from every school in Minnesota came out. One of Dewey's acquaintances was on the Northeast Minnesota Drug Task Force for the State agency giving the report. Each school had the option to disclose the report to the public. The panel recommended that the information be disclosed to the community.

When Satan Came to Moose Lake

The Superintendent of Moose Lake School said "No!" As far as anyone knows nothing was ever done to address the problem. But one thing that everyone did know that if the police catch one of the elite, privileged kids from the community, they were let go. The police learned that they better not make a stink about it or they would be set straight about how they did their police work or they could be administratively dismissed.

He had just read a story in the Duluth News Tribune at the doctor's office in Duluth, which was fifty miles away from Moose Lake. It took place in January of 2007.

A police officer had been hired for the Moose Lake police force. This officer was accused of some wrong doing. It went to trial.

The newspaper did not give a lot of details or give names of the accusers. But it was obvious; someone was out to get him off the police force in Moose Lake.

His lawsuit started in 2001. In the meantime, he could not get a job.

This story about a Moose Lake incident was all over the Duluth papers but nothing was said in either of the two Moose Lake papers. The thinking was to protect the town from scandal.

A Carlton County jury found the officer not guilty. They awarded him the biggest monetary settlement in Carlton County's history. This jury heard all evidence from both sides and determined the officer to be not guilty. These were good honest people. It took six years of a police officer's life to prove his innocence. The officer's name was defamed and his reputation taken away by the Moose Lake rumor mill.

Well, five months later, the not-so-honorable county Judge Wolf in Sheep's Clothing took the jury verdict away from the police officer. The officer appealed the Judge's verdict and won his case against the Judge. But of course, the other side appealed. What will happen? He did not know what happened after that. It had all been kept "hush-hush".

Rumor had it that Judge Wolf in Sheep's Clothing spent a lot of time in Moose Lake. People have said he would walk into the municipal liquor store but be either hauled out for making a ruckus or crawled out.

The "muni" is the biggest city fund raiser. It made so much money; the city razed the old brick building and built a very beautiful aesthetically pleasant, large building right behind the Lutheran Church.

Wow! The joke around town was that a person could have communion every day and night and still walk to church or in some cases crawl. The building looks like a beautiful home. Maybe it has bedrooms where a person can sleep off their intoxication.

The new liquor store had wonderful reviews from the two news papers in town about how beautiful it was and how much money it brought into the city coffers. They did not bother to say a thing about all the broken homes the old "muni" contributed to, all the drunken driving deaths and crippled lives that is caused, the innocent victims of alcoholic beatings, rape, incest, or child abuse that it contributed to. They refused to talk about the cost to society and the tax payer because of the alcohol abuse that comes out of the Moose Lake Municipal Liquor Store and Bar. Of course, if confronted they would say don't blame us everyone else is doing it too. You could say it keeps the hospital in business. But do two wrongs make a right?

The black cloud sent shivers down his spine. It was a constant reminder of both his past situation with the Moose Lake School in 1998 and the direction the community was going. It was not good.

- 15 -

MARRIAGE & THE FAMILY

Dewey was back at the house now eating a quick breakfast. As he looked around, he saw the reminders of his family. He had been greatly blessed. He and his wife had been married for thirty-five years.

Dewey remembered when they were dating. He had known almost immediately that she was the one for him. But you don't meet a girl one month and ask her to get married the next month, especially not this girl.

He finally thought enough time had passed and he was sure she felt the same. The problem was that she would not stop talking long enough for him to pop the question. She would stop to take a breath but by the time he worked up his courage again and got his words set, she was off talking again.

At this rate, they would be eighty-five and still not married. So one night, he finally just "took the bull by the horns" and blurted out "Will you marry me?"

It took her by such surprise, she stopped talking. Her answer was "YES!"

Getting up the courage to ask for her hand in marriage had been a harrowing experience for this quiet, shy farm boy.

Weddings need to be scheduled ahead of time. They did not want to just wake up one day and decide that was the day to get married. So they worked on setting the date.

That was harder than either one of them expected. What would be a good day for a farmer to get married? They decided they wanted to get married in the spring. The date had to be after spring planting and before he had to start haying. It could not be Memorial Day weekend. The only date that seemed to fit was May 20th. So, that was it.

The day finally came. Everything went as planned and the happy couple set off for the honeymoon through the Badlands and Yellowstone National Park. They had a camper on the back of the pickup and camped the whole way. In those days they had to do everything as cheaply as they could.

Another young couple knew they were camping. For their wedding present, they gave them a box of canned camp food. They had taken all the labels off the cans so they had to guess what was inside. They had some interesting meal combos on that trip. They thought one of the cans was dog food but their friends would never say.

After the honeymoon, they returned home to begin everyday life. Prior to their marriage, Dewey had started working at the local feed store. He would make deliveries of feed and fertilizer to the area farmers.

This job gave him the opportunity to get out and meet a lot of people. Lifting all the heavy feed sacks was hard work. Each sack held a hundred pounds of feed. By the end of each day, he had handled about ten tons of feed. It was a good thing he was still in good shape. He also worked within the feed store filling bags, and doing other jobs as needed.

One Saturday the boss, who thought he owned the Co-op Feed Store, had to be gone. As hard as it was for him to let anyone else take over, he decided to put Dewey in charge. The boss was very nervous about leaving someone else in charge. He must have thought he was the only one who could handle all the customers, orders, and the cash register.

The boss never worked alone. There was always one other person to help. But, that weekend Dewey would be working alone.

When the boss picked up the money on Monday, he was sure there had been some troubles. But Dewey had no trouble that day.

When the boss counted up the receipts and the money, he was astonished. It turned out that the Saturday Dewey took over; he had the highest one day sales in the store's history.

The feed store was a good job but it had some draw backs. During the spring and summer, the hours he had to work interfered with farming. His job required him to be away from the farm from eight o'clock in the morning until five or later in the afternoon. That left very little time for plowing, seeding, haying in the summer, and taking care of all the cattle.

The opportunity came up for Dewey to take a part-time school bus driving job for the Moose Lake School. The school bus Supervisor had been asking Dewey many times during the year to come work as a bus driver. He knew about Dewey's past driving experiences in the Army and at St. Cloud. He knew Dewey was a good driver.

He quit his job at the feed store and started out as a substitute driver. He worked his way into a full time job. This only took one year.

He would do the morning bus run. Then he would go home and do the farming until about three o'clock when it was time to do the afternoon route. This gave him the time he needed to get his farm work done and he made more money.

About three years after getting married, they started their family. All together, they had three sons. His boys were a bundle of energy. They were interested in everything.

They loved to collect frogs from the pond. One time they had over forty frogs in a five gallon pail. The youngest one was so proud of the collection. One frog was a gigantic bullfrog about six inches in diameter. The sad part was that by morning, most of the frogs had jumped out of the pail and headed back to the pond.

Climbing was another favorite activity. One day, Dewey looked out the window just in time to see his oldest son, who was only about two years old, climbing to the top of a forty foot grain elevator.

Oh, No! His instinct was to run out and yell for the kid to get down. But since he was standing at the very top, a sudden action could easily make his son fall. So, nonchalantly, Dewey climbed the elevator. As he crawled, he talked calmly so he would not startle the child. Finally he got to the boy, grabbed him and gratefully crawled back down to the ground.

Middle son was not much different. It was nothing to find him hanging upside down by the knees in a tree. When he wasn't doing that he was building wagons and things like that.

The boys all went to school at Moose Lake Public School. They did very well.

During their youth, the boys were all very involved with 4-H in Carlton County just like their Dad. Each one had their special interests including computers, aerospace, sheep, rabbits, and project bowls. They held offices at both the club and county level.

Each one of the boys earned numerous blue ribbons, awards, and the coveted State Fair trips. They all represented the state of Minnesota in Washington, D.C. in a program called Washington Focus. This was a prestigious event and kids had to be selected for this.

Upon graduation, each one went to college to get prepared for their future careers.

Since that time, the boys had all married. They had great jobs. He was very proud of his sons and their families.

- 16 -

THE SPLIT ROCK ROUTE

Dewey had what was called the Split Rock route. He drove that route for fifteen years. During that time he not only got to know the kids very well, he also got to know the parents.

There were several times, when a distraught parent would call him about their child. A situation had come up and they needed advice on how to handle it.

One would think that parents would have taken these matters to the guidance counselor or the Principal. But they didn't. They felt they could trust Dewey's judgment. They had learned from how he dealt with their children, that he had the best interest of the children in mind when he handled the kids.

A lot of them just needed someone to talk to. The School just brushed them off. They wanted to sweep any problems under the carpet and pretend there were no problems. Dewey was willing to take the time to listen to them.

This route was the longest route in the District. The morning and evening route together added up to well over one hundred miles. This was a rural route and just about all of the kids were farm kids. They came from very good, upstanding farm families. Some of the families had as many as twelve kids. On the farthest end of the route, he picked up eighteen kids from just three stops.

Each day Dewey would greet the kids by name as they got on the bus in the morning. In the evening when they got on the bus at the School, he would ask how their day had gone.

Not every day was wonderful. Things happen that really upset kids and they need someone to talk to.

Back in the 1970's there were many kinds of peer pressure that kids encountered. It was a changing time socially. They were exposed to pressure to do drugs. The new movies were very permissive and violent.

A third grader got on the bus one morning eager to tell everyone about the movie he saw the previous night. He told about the "Chainsaw Gang Murders" where a man used a chainsaw to cut up a bunch of women. He gave graphic details about what he saw.

This same boy also brought his "He-Man" toys on the bus. He and the other boys on the bus started acting out scenes and antics from the show. The behavior was so outrageous and violent; Dewey banned these toys after the first week.

The behavior on the buses and in School also became intolerable. Kids were constantly getting hurt as they acted out what they saw on TV. Bus drivers and parents contacted the School about what was happening. It took several months before the School could decide that these "He-Man" characters had to be banned.

At this time the language was changing. It was becoming more profane and vile. On Dewey's bus, bad language was not tolerated. Once in a while it would slip out. When that happened, the kids would apologize. They knew that was the right thing to do and did not argue about it.

The parents backed him up one hundred percent. The parents on the route appreciated how he took care of their kids.

Many times when he would meet them at social events, such as games or concerts, parents would ask "How are things on the route, Dewey?" "Fine, thank you."

They would tell him that if he ever had any trouble with their kids, "he had their permission to give their kids a good hard spanking". He never had to lay a hand on a kid except to give them a hug of encouragement.

Birthdays were special on his route. When a kid had a birthday, he was given a choice. He could have a Happy Birthday Hug or a Happy Birthday Spanking. The girls always picked the hug. Some boys picked the hug, but most of them picked the "spanking". This special event took place at the front of the bus so everyone could see and enjoy the celebration. It was fun. Everyone had a good time.

When it was their birthday, kids brought treats to school. They always made sure to save a lot of treats for Dewey.

The elementary kids outnumbered the high school kids on his bus by about three to one. He could tease them and make the route more fun for him and them.

One day he asked the kids, "What do you like best, riding to school in the morning or riding home in the afternoon?" They all wanted to go home; they didn't want to go to school. They thought that was a dumb question.

Dewey said, "Well, I have to bring you to school for free, so you should pay for your ride home. You should bring me a treat in the morning. I wouldn't have to bring you home for free in the afternoon."

They came up with all kinds of games and silly ideas. It was all to make the time go faster for them. Many of the kids were on the bus for over an hour both in the morning and again in the afternoon.

The next day, Dewey had forgotten all about the treat idea. He had just been kidding with them and did not mean it seriously.

The very first stop was at a family with six kids. They each had a little package that they handed him. One was a hamburger; one was fries, melted malt, and three cookies. The malt was still cold so he started sipping on that until he got to the next stop.

That stop also had six kids. They had one bag for the whole family. It contained an egg sandwich and a can of pop.

Just about every stop on the rest of the route gave him something. He had food stored on top of the heater console, on the floor next to the gear shift, and next to his seat.

The kids were just beaming over the thought that they brought all this food for their bus driver. They knew he was just kidding about paying for their ride home in the evening, but they all thought bringing him food for pay was a fun idea.

They used to count telephone poles. He also tried to get them to count fence posts, but they went by too fast.

One fall the deer were very plentiful. There was a big corn field where they would gather. Every afternoon when the bus came, the deer started running in the same direction the bus was going.

They had a contest to count to see how many deer were in the herd. The kids came up with every kind of number. They did that for many days.

To change the contest, Dewey said, "By this time, you have probably noticed that some deer have brown eyes and some have blue eyes. I want you to count only the deer that have one brown eye and one blue eye. Look closely."

Of course, the high school kids knew he was just kidding. But they had a good time listening to the little kids.

The little kids would squint and look to try to find the right deer. They would comment "They only have brown eyes."

Then Dewey would say, "See the one with the broken horn?" At forty miles an hour, it would be hard to make out details of any kind, let alone count them. But it sure kept those little kids busy.

All these games and fun ideas were how they became one big family.

One year Dewey and his family grew a lot of pumpkins. Just before Halloween, they harvested the pumpkins and lined them up in the yard. He had raised the pumpkins just for his bus kids.

On an afternoon route, shortly before Halloween, Dewey pulled the bus into his yard before bringing the kids home. He told them they could each pick out the pumpkin of their choice.

The high school kids took small pumpkins. The little kids took the biggest pumpkins they couldn't carry. It was so much fun. Some even picked a pumpkin for a younger brother or sister.

The bus was so full of kids and pumpkins they could hardly get down the aisle. The big kids enjoyed helping the little kids get off the bus with their huge pumpkins.

They did that for several years. The great pumpkin patch was later replaced by a "black cow" picnic.

Every year it was customary for bus drivers to treat the bus kids on the last day of school. For a few years Dewey took the kids to the Dairy Queen. That was fun, but very expensive for a young family man back in the '70's and '80's. He couldn't even afford to take his own family to the Dairy Queen much less sixty-five bus kids. He had to find a cheaper way to picnic.

He asked the kids "How would you like to have a "black cow" picnic this year? It will be something different." They were not very enthused about that; mainly because they had no idea what that was.

They did know he was raising Black Angus cows. The high school kids said, "Yeah, let's have a black cow picnic (thinking they were getting hamburgers)."

Usually Dewey did not have the treat on the very last day of school because many kids did not ride the bus that day. He wanted all the kids to take part in the treat, so he would have it at least a week before school was out.

They needed a warm day for a "black cow" picnic. They pulled into Dewey's farm yard. The yard was filled with picnic tables set up on the lawn. The tables had big paper cups, pails of ice cream, and gallons of root beer.

Dewey scooped the ice cream into the cups. His wife poured the root beer over the ice cream. The kids lined up and were just so surprised about what a "black cow" was. They had never heard a root beer float being called a black cow.

They were told to keep their cups because they had to keep coming back for more until all the ice cream and root beer were gone. This is why he had to have it on a warm day.

You've never seen sixty more well behaved and appreciative kids than the ones on his bus route that day. Every year after that, they asked "Are we going to have a "black cow" picnic this year?"

- 17 -

THE KETTLE RIVER ROUTE

When the senior most driver retired, Dewey had the opportunity to get that route. This one was the shortest route.

He thought it might be a nice challenge to try a short route. After all, he was second in seniority after his friend, Harold.

He later discovered that this would turn out to be the biggest mistake of his life. The extra time he gained from having the shorter route was definitely not worth the problems that arose. But that comes later.

The Kettle River route was more of a challenge than he ever imagined. The previous bus driver was so close to retirement that he did not bother with any discipline. He just let the kids run wild.

There were many feuding parents that Dewey had not known about. The diversity of people was a real challenge.

He found the parents would not communicate with each other. Instead of taking care of problems between neighbor kids themselves, they just let the problems escalate. Then it exploded on the bus. However, they soon did develop a measure of trust in Dewey. He took care of their kids. He was fair.

He had four high school E.B.D. kids at one time. They were totally out of control with parents and School authorities.

Usually, one E.B.D. kid was all a bus driver could handle. Four of these kids were just too much. They would start a fight or swear up a storm, even hurting little kids. The School refused to put an aide on the bus to help with discipline.

He could not tell you how many times he had to stop the bus to break up a fight and separate kids. Everyday he wrote up a report, brought it to the Principal, and hoped for some action.

It should be noted here that when the drivers brought these kids to School, another bus would take all the E.B.D. kids from Moose Lake and Barnum up to Cloquet. This town was twenty-five miles away. Here they had special teachers to teach these kids proper behavior.

Oh yeah! That bus had an aid to help keep them from hurting each other. Dewey's bus route had sixty-nine kids on a seventy-two passenger bus. He had no help with the kids as he drove his twenty-five miles twice a day.

Dewey had some very graphic episodes on the bus and for all his efforts to keep order; the Principal said that he could not assign seats to any child. Assigning seats would discriminate and violate their rights.

Permissive behavior was considered acceptable to the School. There were not fair consequences given for bad behavior. If a child from a "well-to-do" or "in" family got into trouble, the whole matter was covered over and no significant consequence was given. It did not matter how serious the bad behavior was.

However, if a child from a poor or not-so-popular family got into trouble, no matter how small, the School would throw the book at the kid.

Early one morning, a near tragedy took place. As Dewey was approaching the main bus stop in Kettle River, one of the boys deliberately pushed the little special needs boy right in front of the wheels of the bus.

Dewey slammed on the brakes, stopping inches from the child. The child's mother was at the bus stop and ran over to help her child up and into the bus. She looked at him and asked, "Did you see what happened?"

Dewey confirmed exactly what happened and told her he would be writing up the boy who pushed her child into the street. He made sure the little fellow was alright and continued his route.

As soon as he got to the School, Dewey wrote up the boy who did the pushing. This boy knew exactly what would happen if Dewey could not get the bus stopped and he pushed that child into the street anyway. This was serious enough of a situation to consider it attempted murder. Yet the boy showed no remorse for what he did.

Dewey waited for the results of the paperwork he had turned in. Days went by and nothing happened. The naughty boy was still on the bus.

Dewey started asking questions. This was when he found out that the Principal did not believe Dewey's account of what happened. He shared this information with the parent of the little boy. She was infuriated.

She took it upon herself to write a letter explaining that she was at the bus stop and saw the whole incident. What she said confirmed what Dewey's report said. Still nothing happened.

They found out that neither her letter nor Dewey's report had been believed. Finally, the Principal interviewed the kids at the bus stop. Most of them confirmed what the two adults involved had stated. The others said they had not seen what happened. The Principal was a close friend to the parents of the naughty boy and refused take any action. He just shoved it under the carpet.

The parent of the special needs boy went to the Superintendent and the School Board. Absolutely nothing was done about an incident that could have resulted in the maiming or death of a little boy.

Prior to this time, the State approved the "Open Enrollment" legislation. Kids in the Moose Lake School District could go to a different school and vice-versa. Due to the many problems at Moose Lake, many of the Kettle River area parents decided to take advantage of this option.

Busses from four schools came into the Moose Lake School District to pick up students to take back to their schools. They were Barnum, Cromwell, McGregor, and Willow River.

Open enrollment gave parents a choice about where to send their children. It also meant that Moose Lake would lose about five thousand dollars of state aid for each child that went to another school.

All of the routes lost a few kids. But Moose Lake School administration and the Board would never admit that the way they dealt with students and their problems had anything to do with the decline in student enrollment.

There was a young family of six kids on Dewey's route. One little seventh grade girl was being picked on by a big Kettle River girl. He talked to both parents on the phone about the girls leaving each other alone.

The big girl kept on picking on the little girl. The little girl had been told by her mother to just do nothing. She was told to just sit in her seat and not talk or look at the big girl. That infuriated the big girl even more.

Every day, there were also things happening in the School between the two girls. Nothing was being done about this situation.

One afternoon the big girl got on the bus and went right over to the other girl and started beating on her. Dewey got the big girl off the bus and called on his radio for help.

When he had his back turned, that big girl got back on the bus and started beating on the little girl again. This time, the little girl came up with a right punch to the mouth. Then it became a real "cat" fight and became difficult to separate them.

A Principal came nonchalantly over to the bus. Dewey told him to take the big girl. He was not going to take her on the route. He said, "Have her parents come and get her!"

He got a call from both parents that night. He told the big girl's parents what she had done. That parent would not accept what her girl did. She refused to believe him. The parent said her daughter was banned from School for a day and that was not fair.

The little girl's parent was very concerned about the safety of her daughter. Her daughter had received a threatening call from the other girl saying she was going to get beat up if she came to School the next day. Dewey asked if she had called the Principal to let him know about this. She said she had.

The next morning, when he brought the kids to School, he told the little girl to be careful. He told her to go talk to the Principal about the threat.

She did not get that far. There were some friends of the big girl who met her at her locker.

It was about eleven o'clock in the morning when Dewey got a call from the little girl's mother. She asked, "Will you please come over to our house?"

She had taken all six of the kids out of School. The little girl was battered all over the body. She was swollen in the face. She had been kicked and smashed into the lockers. She had been knocked to the floor. No one would even help her.

There were three girls beating up on one tiny little seventh grade girl. The Principal did absolutely nothing – not one thing about this situation. He did not even get medical treatment for the little girl.

The mother said, "I am leaving this area. I quit my job this morning. Even Los Angeles, where I came from, isn't as bad as Moose Lake."

The black cloud is getting thicker.

One of the other students that should have been on Dewey's route was traumatized so badly at School that her parents sent her to Barnum. At this School she was treated kindly and fairly. She was given a chance to succeed. Her grades improved. She gained enough self-confidence that she was able to become a cheerleader. She had her life back again.

In the small town of Kettle River, he picked up about twenty of the kids on his route. The rest of the route was the rural kids. The rural kids and the town kids did not get along. It was a constant battle.

There were more than enough stories about abuse and unfairness in the Moose Lake School to fill another book. They even had a gun incident.

It is a tragedy to raise kids in a terrorist environment like this. Our own kids went through some bad experiences, but not as bad as most.

The community was very permissive. They allowed heavy drinking and bad language. It really showed up in the kids; only they exaggerated the behaviors even more.

This all led to more sexual promiscuity, abortions, sexual diseases, and alcoholism. Nearly everyone who played baseball had a wad in their mouth. They thought it was cool.

But how as a parent, teacher, or civic leader could they say anything when they were doing the same bad things their kids were doing? It got to the point that if they were to remain "friends" with their kids, they had to back up their kid's bad behavior. The saying "Boys will be boys" was rampant.

It was during this time of permissiveness that parents looked to alternative schooling. Christian schools were started. Those who lived too far away or could not afford the tuition, home schooled their children. They had to protect their children somehow.

By this time, he should have seen some hand writing on the wall. But he was just too busy with so many extra curricular trips, farming, and raising their three sons to see where it was all headed.

- 18 -

UNCLE LOUIS' FUNERAL

While Dewey was still driving the Kettle River route, a very unpleasant situation arose. At first it seemed quite ordinary. The way the Superintend chose to handle it, turned out to be anything but ordinary.

Dewey and his family got word that Uncle Louie had been killed in a terrible tractor accident. This took place up on his farm in Goodland, Minnesota. That town was over in the Grand Rapids and Swan River area.

All his life, Uncle Louie had been a very hard worker. However, he also had a reputation for loving the homemade brew that was so common in his area of the country. This made life difficult for his family.

Uncle Louie met the Lord. His days of drinking ended quickly. That helped the family run more smoothly and gave more money to make ends meet.

Uncle Louie continued to love life and live life to the fullest. He just did not need alcohol anymore. He was a lot more fun to be with. If there was a crowd of people, Louie was in the middle. He was a good family man. If a person needed help for anything, Louie was there.

The funeral was going to be held in the morning. It was about an eighty mile drive. So Dewey asked his Supervisor if he could take the day off for a funeral. He was told, "Sure, if you train in the sub for your route."

He had one of the most complicated routes in the District. Every other day he took one road and some days he took a different road. It all depended on the classes and ages of the kids riding the bus as well as where that kid lived.

The kindergartners went every other day. Then there were a lot of broken homes where mom got the child one day and the next day dad got them. Also, there were the days the babysitter got them and some days even gramma got them.

If that wasn't confusing enough, some of the kids had Girl Scouts or Boy Scouts. Of course, the child would get confused about where he should go. Dewey was expected to know so he could deliver the kid to the correct location.

If children had to ride a different bus, they had to have a note giving permission, signed by a parent. Sometimes the drivers got a forgery and they had to deal with that. This would hold up the route and in the evening the kids wanted to get home right away. There was a lot of pressure put on the bus driver to get going.

Well, his sub rode two mornings and two afternoons to learn his route. He called Dewey the night before the funeral. He said that he just didn't think he could do the morning route but he would do the afternoon route because it was easier.

That was true. The kids would never send a driver down the wrong way in the afternoon like they would in the morning. Most kids are good and honest about helping but, in the morning if it is a kid they don't particularly like, they might say to skip a road. Of course, that would make the kid's mom and dad mad and they would call the School. The

Supervisor would then say "What are you listening to the kids for?" Then the teacher and the Principal would be mad for making the kid late.

To make things easier, Dewey agreed to do the morning route. After the route, he picked up his wife and they rushed off to Goodland. They got to the funeral a bit late and felt real bad about that. It disrupts the service when someone comes in late.

It was such a sad funeral. The whole family was very distraught. The minister shared what had happened.

Uncle Louie was bringing a load of wood to the yard. He apparently had a heart attack. As he slumped over the steering wheel, the tractor kept going and hit the house. The force of the hit on the house bumped him off the seat and he fell in front of the spinning tractor tire.

It shredded him up until his wife and daughter came home from shopping. For the family to come home and find their loved one in that terrible shape was very traumatic.

Dewey and his wife spent the day with the family and went home. It was good to spend that time with Uncle Louie's family, but so sad.

The next day, his Supervisor had him sign a funeral leave paper for the half day off. The day after that, the Supervisor came and said that uncles were not covered in funeral leave. He gave him a choice. He could take sick leave or personal leave.

Dewey chose the sick leave. The following day he was told that this was all coming from the Superintendent, Ricky. He was told he could not take sick leave; that he must take a full day of personal leave.

He thought "Why is all this happening?" So he contacted the Union Representative. The Union Representative sent a letter to Mr. Ricky. Then Mr. Ricky said Dewey had to take half a day of personal leave.

Dewey then sent a letter to the Superintendent saying that since they only got two personal days a year he needed them later for personal business. He would just not charge the District anything for his half day at the funeral.

His Supervisor told him a day or so later that they had to meet with Mr. Ricky the next morning.

The next day when they met, Mr. Ricky asked Dewey very sarcastically why he had gone to a funeral that was not acceptable under the contract.

Dewey said no one knew the contract said that an employee could not go to a funeral of an uncle. The business manager got the contract out after the fact and was making a big deal out of nothing.

Dewey told Mr. Ricky he would not charge anything, thinking that would make every body happy. To him it wasn't the money, it was the time off. Besides he had the maximum 125 days of sick leave accrued for years. He said, "If you want to make a big deal of it I won't charge anything."

Mr. Ricky jumped out of his chair and came over to Dewey just screaming obscenities at him. He thought sure he was going to beat him up. Mr. Ricky turned beet red and just shook with anger and hate.

Janet, the business manager, was not done. She kept the controversy going and changed the rules and the interpretation of the contract.

Finally, Dewey said, "Do whatever you want to do. If you want to bill me for going to an uncle's funeral, so be it."

He thought he had seen the lowest pit of disrespect for a grieving person until his Mom died. He had a new Supervisor. Dewey was very distraught from the funeral. In addition to that, he was the executor of the estate. Everything was dumped on him at one time, with no help from any of his siblings.

After the funeral, he asked his Supervisor for a second day off. The Supervisor said to take what ever time he needed. So, Dewey filled out a two day request for funeral leave.

Oh boy! All "hell" broke loose. He was summoned to the main office just three days after burying his Mom. Janet chewed him out, up one side and down the other, because the contract allowed only one day for his mother's funeral.

He said, "Well, I was pretty sick after the funeral and didn't think I could drive my kids very safely in that condition."

Being sick in this instance was not acceptable because he had gone to someone's funeral. He argued that this was not just "someone," it was his Mom..

Finally, he said, "Well send me a bill for how much I owe you."

She threatened, "You can be fired for these kinds of things."

"You mean I can be fired for going to my Mom's funeral?"

"No, for breaking a contract!"

Dewey never carried a contract around. He just thought some human dignity would kick in during a hard time. Besides, no one else knew this either. It seemed it was always only after your bad deed was done that anything was ever said. Many of these kinds of things happened to a lot of employees through the years.

Dewey remembered that when he talked to Principals, Superintendents, and Board members of other schools about these issues, they were flabbergasted at how hateful someone could be.

It was common knowledge that if one of the surrounding school districts teamed up with Moose Lake, they would be demeaned in some way to show the superiority and power of Moose Lake.

For a town of just twelve hundred people, it didn't seem they had anything to be superior about. Oops! He was wrong. They had a superior meanness.

For thirty years Moose Lake had been trying to become a "Minnesota Star City." However, most people "in the know" know they really do not deserve it.

- 19 -

ALLEN

Allen was a really good, honest, hard working man. He grew up in the neighboring community of Askov. He married and moved to Kansas. There they started to raise a beautiful family.

He worked for a large corporation doing electrical repair. Allen had a natural talent for repairing electrical appliances such as TVs. If you could plug it in, he could fix it..

Allen always had a great desire to own his own business and be his own boss. Finally, he bundled up his wife and three young kids and moved to Moose Lake.

Allen was a very committed and devout Christian. He believed in the saving grace of JESUS, the gift of eternal life, and salvation through repentance of his sin. He raised his family with that belief.

Allen was a great spiritual leader in his Church. He was a respected community leader. He held no official city post, but when they needed electronic work, Allen was the one they called.

He bought an old cement block building in downtown Moose Lake. The family was able to live upstairs. Allen had his repair shop downstairs.

He started selling a few name brand appliances. He had a couple TVs, a few washers, and some dryers. It was just too cramped for space. If you wanted something different from what he had, you could order what you wanted.

After getting well settled, Allen agonized over buying a real nice building with lots of room. It had more room than he needed but it was on main street.

Well, he bought it and made a deal with the carpet man who was also Allen's good friend. They had A & L TV and JIM'S Carpet & Furniture in the same building.

Allen was beginning to experience a trend in America. In a lot of cases it was cheaper to throw the appliance away than to fix it. You could go to Wal-Mart and buy cheaper.

It also took a lot of time to track down a replacement for a component that did not work. It also took a goodly amount of time to take the item apart to get at the "inerds".

Allen decided to take on a part-time bus driver job for the Moose Lake School. He needed the insurance. After so many months of probation, he would get health insurance for his family.

Allen was a very quiet spoken man. He never raised his voice. Dewey never saw him get angry at anyone. He never used foul language. It seemed that his bosses at the School took that as an expression of weakness. But Allen was not a weak person. His walk with GOD made him strong.

One time Superintendent Ricky called Allen into his office and made some accusations about his work on the bus route. The allegations were totally untrue and Allen told him so. Mr. Ricky, or as the community called him "the old goat" said, "Okay choir boy; I don't want to see you in here again".

Unknown to the majority of people was the fact that there was a subtle push to get rid of Christian drivers and replace them with JWs (Jehovah's Witnesses).

Allen needed a short route so he could get back to the store and work late every night. The School refused to give him insurance on a short route. They would not even give him partial insurance.

The School finally agreed to split the route with a sub driver. The sub could only drive mornings because of his regular job. That was great for both of them. It would work best for Allen to drive afternoons but he still had no insurance.

Allen loved the kids on his route very much. He drove an eighty passenger bus; hauling mainly urban kids whose parents thought they could do no wrong. It was a short route.

The kids found out how far they could go when their parents stood up for them when they were caught being naughty.

For the idea that Johnny and Sally could do no wrong, society is reaping the rewards today. Parents like this are the direct cause of the decline in American values today.

Of course the Principal and Superintendent wanted to support these kinds of parents because they had the same way of raising their own children.

The kids on his bus were getting a stronger and stronger foot hold. They would make absurd and ridiculous complaints about their drivers. They cut the seats, marked up the walls, and would run up and down the aisle. If the drivers stopped the bus to get control, the students would open the windows and scream obscenities.

No matter how many times the drivers complained NO action was taken. Did you know that no school bus driver had any authority to discipline? Drivers were to only report what took place. At least, that was the way it was at the Moose Lake School.

One day Dewey heard that Allen and the other driver had been terminated. He was shocked. He was curious about this so he asked to meet with both of them.

Dewey asked to see their dismissal papers. They had not been given any. He then asked, "What did the Superintendent tell you?" They said that they never got to see him. They said it was the Supervisor who told them they had no job any more.

Dewey told them that he believed it was against the law to just fire a person with no reason given. Then they began to realize that what was happening was not fair. They should have the right to defend themselves, after all this is America, right?

Allen was a veteran of the Vietnam War. Under the Minnesota state laws he had rights he did not know about.

The plot thickened and got even dirtier. Past practice for the District was to hire the next senior sub driver for a regular route. They were going to hire one person for that route. The guy was well qualified and had been a sub for over two years. He wanted to move up.

The Superintendent made the Supervisor advertise the position in the paper. Dewey read the ad in the paper and told Allen, "Under the circumstances, you probably won't get the job, but why don't both of you apply for the job and see what happens?"

So that is what they did. It ended up that there were four applicants. There was Allen, his driving partner, the long term sub, and a young fellow who was working as a bus driver for Barnum. This was a school just five miles away.

Of all four of the drivers, the one from Barnum had the least experience. However, the rest of the drivers all saw what was coming. The hand writing was on the wall. There was a standing joke all over town. Who is going to be the next JW bus driver for Moose Lake School?

What administration did to decide who to give the job to had never been done before. They set up a test for each driver to take. The three Moose Lake drivers thought it would be a written drivers test, sort of a refresher test. Instead, it was a timed test given by the Supervisor and the test had nothing to do with driving. It did take a lot of thinking. It was a hard test plus being timed made it harder.

Mr. JW, from Barnum, finished the test way ahead of the others. The other guys could not believe he got done so quickly.

Allen had a college degree and had taken many tests in his life. None of the other candidates had the education he had. They all finished the test and wanted to know the results.

They were told the Superintendent would go over the tests and make a decision soon. The next morning the JW was on the job driving for Moose Lake and the senior ranking sub was sent to Barnum to do the JW's route there.

Allen was curious about the test and asked the Supervisor about the results. He was told the JW got 100 and he was next with around 90. He wondered "How in the world did the JW get 100 and in such a short time?"

Allen told Dewey he couldn't believe it when the Supervisor said, "Well, he had all the answers." And then he just laughed. They knew the Superintendent had made up the test and given the JW the answer key.

It was a very devastating blow to Allen to be mistreated so badly. He took it as a direct reflection on his character and reputation as an honest man. Both he and his partner felt publicly humiliated.

Remember this was a small town where everyone knew everyone. The Superintendent fired these two honest, well respected community people. They must be guilty of something, right? If the School made a claim about a person, it must be true – right? That is how the people in a small community think.

The people should have known this was not so. Why didn't the good people of Moose Lake stand up and help defend the truth of an honest man? Shame on the people of Moose Lake!

Very shortly after this, Allen got very sick. He was diagnosed with a very fast spreading cancer. Allen was given six months to live.

He knew he did not have the money for a funeral. He feared leaving his family with a great debt. He was not even going to have treatment for his cancer to try to save money.

Just before all the skullduggery of the school, Allen and his wife fell in love with a young foster boy. Now he was concerned that his widow would also have a toddler to raise alone.

No one can tell how many times Allen dropped what he was doing to go fix computer problems at the Moose Lake School. When no one at the School could figure out the problem, Allen could. He even took care of the problems in the main office and for the Superintendent.

Someone, and nobody to this day knows who it was, sent Allen a copy of the Veterans Preference Law. It showed that he had a right to a hearing. With the help of his pastor, he got an attorney to represent him. He charged the School with unlawful firing.

Allen was very sick by this time. He hoped he would at least get a large enough money settlement to cover a cheap funeral. His goal was to not saddle the family with a funeral expense.

The School was represented by Krumson Associates of Edina, Minnesota. They had a reputation for being unscrupulous, underhanded, threatening, lying, mean, vindictive, and hurtful.

Most school districts in Minnesota had hired Krumson at one time. Just about all of them had quit their association with them because of their dishonest services and cruel treatment of honest people. Moose Lake School to this day has the Krumson firm on retainer.

Basically, Krumson was a full time employee of the School. They did every thing in their power to win.

The evidence against the School was so overwhelming; the Judge awarded Allen a $10,000 award, enough to cover the funeral. The School's attorney screamed obscenities at Allen. He just cursed him relentlessly. The Judge gave strict orders that the School was to get the money to Allen right away.

One of the times Allen went to the hospital, Dewey went to visit him. Allen asked him to take the TV off the wall and put it on the bed so he could fix it.

Dewey said, "Are you kidding?"

"No. This will be my third one. It just takes a little longer now."

Of course he did not charge for the service. And of course, he got no discount on his hospital bill either.

Time was now very near for Allen to meet his Lord. There was no more fixing TVs, going out on service calls, or getting satellites set up in below zero temperatures in January so people could watch the Super Bowl.

The doctors said he had about a week to live. Every day he would ask his wife "Did the check come?"

Allen always gave freely of his time and talents. He loved to sing in the choir at church. He had a good sense of humor and a nice laugh.

Allen held on to the thread of life, did the check come yet? Did the check come? Did the check come?

Allen struggled but his time ran out. But no, the check did not come.

Three days before his death his wife called the Judge to tell him that Allen's check never came. The Judge was infuriated that his order to the School was not carried out.

But the day Allen died; a check was sent and received. It was addressed to the ESTATE of Allen.

There was no estate. The family had to go through all kinds of legal procedures and expense to get the money out of the estate so Allen's wife could pay the funeral.

To Dewey that was done with extreme hatred and malice. Every one of the School Board members, Superintendent, and lawyers who took part in Allen's death will one day stand before GOD and His judgment seat.

Knowing Allen, this is what he would say, "I forgive you for you know not what you do. Repent of your sin and be made whole. Ask in JESUS' name for forgiveness of your sins. For JESUS died on the cross for your sins. AMEN."

Salvation – it is offered to the most sinful. Some verses that will help you, the reader, understand are: Isaiah.1:8, 1 John 1:9, Luke 19:10, Isaiah.44:22 Isaiah. 43:25, 1 John 2; 1-2, and Romans 10:13.

- 20 -

SATAN COMES TO MOOSE LAKE

In Kettle River there was a stop in town that consisted of about eleven kids. These were mostly elementary age kids.

The first to get off all the time was a severely handicapped child. He could get down the steps without help; he just needed the time to do it.

One evening, as they got to the bus stop the kids all lined up in the aisle. All of a sudden, the front kids were being pushed up tight. The little handicapped child was hanging on for dear life with one hand. He was losing his balance and screaming bloody murder.

A fourth grade hellion at the back of the row put his shoulder against the kid in front of him and acted like a bulldozer pushing everyone out the door.

It happened so fast, Dewey barely had time to put his hand back to stop the boy from pushing. The handicapped boy had fallen to the floor at the top of the stairs. By this time, he was being helped to his feet. He was helped the rest of the way down the steps by two kids behind him.

Dewey wrote up a report to give to the Principal in the morning. He put his bus away and went home.

About ten minutes later, the Sheriff came to his house. He said they got a report that he beat up a little fourth grade boy.

Dewey said, "Well, that would be a lie."

The Sheriff said, "Kids do not lie." Dewey could tell he was mad.

Dewey and his wife just stood there shocked by what the Sheriff had just said. With his years of dealing with kids on bus routes and his wife's experiences in education for twenty-five years, they knew full well that children do lie, especially to keep out of bigger trouble.

The Sheriff said that the parents had pressed charges against Dewey with the Carlton County Court for beating up their son.

This incident took place at a time when many people believed anything and everything that kids said. If you were an adult involved, you had absolutely no credibility. Many people went to jail on false charges made by kids.

Remember all the daycare providers that went to jail? Years later, after the kids grew up they could assess what the adults had told them to say. They realized that what they said were lies that had sent innocent people to jail. Many of these people were finally released after spending time in jail for things they had not done.

The next morning, Dewey went to the bus garage as usual. His Supervisor told him he was being put on administrative leave for beating up on a fourth grade boy. Dewey said he didn't beat up on anyone.

The Supervisor refused to look at his report on the incident. When Dewey brought it to the Principal, he would not see him. He claimed to be too busy. So Dewey was sent home for the rest of the school year, which was three days.

Dewey then learned that the Superintendent had chosen not to make a decision on this situation. He was still in charge of the School until July 1st, even though he was leaving. Instead, he gave the case over to the incoming Superintendent, Dr. Moldy. She actually had no legal authority yet. But, she took the liberty of making a decision anyway. This turned out to be a hint of things to come.

Without reading Dewey's report or even meeting him and talking to him personally, she had made a decision that he should be placed on this leave.

The news of his being put on administrative leave without being given a chance to tell his side of the story shocked Dewey.

Dewey was frustrated. He knew he had done nothing wrong. He decided to call the chairman of the School Board. In this conversation, he told what really happened. He even offered to bring his bus down to the School and show everyone how the situation had played out. The chairman refused to allow any evidence to be given by Dewey.

Whatever he tried fell on deaf ears. It seemed that no one would help him. Not one person from the School wanted to see Dewey's written report about the incident.

Then something miraculous was beginning to unfold. The kids told their parents what happened. After all, they were the witnesses to what happened.

The kids got a petition to bring Dewey back. The parents wrote letters to the Superintendent, the Principal, and the School Board.

In spite of what the kids and parents did, administration did absolutely nothing to help Dewey.

He found out that the bratty fourth grader's parents were best friends of the Principal. Discipline of any kind was not tolerated by either of them. It was the proverbial "my kid can do no wrong".

At the time, Dewey's best friend was the Under Sheriff of Carlton County. He asked his friend what he should do. His friend asked him if he gave a report about what happened.

He said that he had written one up but no one would take it. He was concerned because the County Attorney was supposed to decide what to do about the case. The parents of the fourth grader had filed charges against him for beating up their child.

Dewey asked his friend when he would ever get to tell his side of the story. His friend said all too often that is the case. Only one side gets heard and a decision is made from the information from only one side of a story.

He said the people involved cannot even see the County Attorney themselves. He offered to give the County Attorney a copy of Dewey's testimony.

The School would not give Dewey the testimony that parents had given about him. But in spite of the School's attitude, he had almost 100% support of his bus kids and their parents.

Some parents went to the Sheriff's department on Dewey's behalf. You see, the other bus kids saw the rascal fourth grader actually get hurt on a playground in Kettle River and not by their bus driver.

Since Dewey was relieved of his job until the School could trump up the charges against him, the kids missed out on the annual end of the year picnic. Of course, the School could not care less.

The School Board, at the recommendation of the Superintendent, came up with an order of importance. It was the Superintendent first, Principal next, then teachers, and so on down the line making the bus drivers last.

The School delighted in calling the bus drivers uncertified. They stressed that whenever they referred to bus drivers. It was as if they were the lowliest scum on the earth.

In order to be a bus driver, a person had to have a special bus driving license. They also had to pass a physical and pass drug and alcohol testing all on their own time. A person had to be a licensed bus driver in order to drive for any district - that does not sound "uncertified".

The Moose Lake bus drivers drove a combined 150,000 miles a year. They had to learn CPR and take many classes on driving related issues. Still the Moose Lake School Board had the gall to call a bus driver uncertified.

They tried to compare the drivers to the teachers. To compare two vocations of a different nature was comparing apples to oranges.

As bus drivers, they had the lives of all the District kids in their hands every day. But the disrespectful way the School treated some of the drivers the way they did was purely criminal.

The summer dragged by for Dewey as he waited for a response from the County Attorney. Would he go to trial? Would the Sheriff show up at his door to put him in jail? It was agonizing!

In the mean time, everyone all over the place heard that Dewey, the bus driver, beat up a kid. A few people came to his door to hear his side of what happened. He could tell some would not believe him because they were friends of the culprit. At least they gave him a chance to speak.

Just days before School started in the fall, Dewey got a letter from the School. It said that he was reinstated and could start his route for the fall.

He found out that the letter from the County Attorney had been sent to the School back in June when the case was dropped. But the Moose Lake School had let him worry for two extra months before telling him the news. This was in spite of the many calls he had made to the Principal. It was pretty dirty on the part of the Principal, Superintendent, and School Board.

Dewey called the County Attorney the day he found this out. He asked if he could meet with him personally. The County Attorney agreed to a meeting and they met the next day.

Dewey brought his wife with. After that he brought her with for every meeting so he would have a witness to what was said.

The County Attorney was very kind. He was very surprised that Dewey just got notice of the charges being dropped. He told Dewey that his reputation has been tarnished.

The County Attorney said that the School had given Dewey no defense or help in spite of all he had done for the School all those years.

However, he had received all these letters from parents and kids on his route. He also had read the description Dewey wrote about what happened.

The County Attorney said "YOU SHOULD HAVE BEEN GIVEN A MEDAL FOR WHAT YOU DID IN THAT SITUATION!"

He said that there was a lot of support for him and all the evidence was against the fourth grader. He said that he had the family in the office and showed them the evidence against the boy.

Then the boy admitted that he lied because he didn't like the bus driver. The boy said he had really gotten skun up on the playground in Kettle River after Dewey dropped him off. He went home and told his mommy that the bad old bus driver beat him up and that was a lie. Other kids had also said that the boy had gotten hurt on the playground.

The County Attorney told the parents they needed to send an apology to Mr. Anderson for the tarnished reputation they caused. They promised they would do that and they would also apologize to the School.

The County Attorney asked, "Did you get the apology?"

"NO, I DID NOT."

"I'm sorry!" he said. "Some people are like that. They told me they did not want you to lose your job."

Dewey had not heard this story until the County Attorney told him. He was surprised that a lie could go so far.

There never was an apology from the parents or even the School. When Dewey ran his bus route, if a kid offended someone, they had to apologize. Ninety-nine percent of the kids had enough respect for him to obey the rules.

Even after a time the E.B.D. kids could see the error of their ways. Most of the problems came from the upbringing in the home. They were raised with no discipline and no expectations. That tells a kid there is no love or caring.

To solve the discipline problems the parent, with the help of the School hauled the kid to a doctor. He said the kid had ADHD and started the kid on a heavy drug program. What a farce. And who suffered from all these drugs? The kid, with a lazy parent that refused to learn how to be a parent, was the one who suffered. He still thought no one really cared about him, but now he was on drugs.

It is a proven fact now that it is the parenting that screwed up these kids. Oh but heaven forbid that you should pray for your kid. With the highest teen suicide rate in history going on now, don't you think it is time people wake up?

Dewey's situation showed a long continuous and persistent history of unjust decisions being made against good honest people. The Moose Lake School was operating just like a drunk that never sobers up. Things just continued to get worse. When the next person took over, they did even more hurtful things and more lives were ruined.

But just like the drunk who never gets hurt, those in authority are seldom held accountable for the evil they have done. Outsiders looking in were too blind to see it. The ones on the inside were afraid to risk their position by revealing the truth.

Dewey had no idea that his situation was just a taste of what the Superintendent had in store for him and many other people. Looking back, he realized that was truly the day that Satan had come to Moose Lake.

- 21 -

TO RUSSIA WITH LOVE

Dewey had no way of knowing that years before Satan arrived in Moose Lake, things were setting up in his life that would lead to very difficult days.

It all really started one fall day in 1994. Dewey was sitting in his living room reading the latest copy of *The Successful Farmer*.

He noticed an article about a young farm family from Wisconsin who was doing missionary work in Russia through the Fellowship of Christian Farmers International. He was fascinated by the story and pictures.

When he got to the bottom of the article, he saw that FCFI needed farmers for a trip that was being planned for the following July.

He asked his wife if she wanted to go to Russia. She said "yes" but thought there was no way that they would be accepted. After all, they were just small farmers from Northern Minnesota. She could not imagine actually going to Russia. "Oh, ye of little faith!" God was saying.

Early in January, they received the news that they had been accepted. Now it was a busy time getting everything in order. They needed birth certificates, passports, and to make plans for their three boys to take over the farm at the height of the haying season.

They were excited as they planned the trip. They went to all kinds of companies and organizations to get donations of caps, soaps, toothpaste, and so forth that they could give to the Russian people. Everyone was very generous.

Finally, they had two large duffle bags and two carry-on bags all packed and ready. They were off to Chicago's O'Hare Airport to meet the other farmers making the trip.

In all there were six farmers heading to Russia. They came from all parts of the country. Except for Dewey and his wife, they all had much larger farming operations.

Ten hours later, they landed at Moscow International Airport. This was a rude awakening to the culture difference. The airport was where international heads-of-state came into Russia. Yet what greeted the arriving farmers was a dark, dank, smelly room that was filled with cigarette smoke. They had been herded like cattle from the plane to this point.

Customs went well due to the young Russian fellow they had met in Chicago. He was heading home for the first time in five years. He understood Russian and was able to help with the custom processes.

The farmers were met by the travel agent and brought to a domestic airport. Here they boarded another plane for St. Petersburg.

When they arrived in St. Petersburg, they met the missionary family and one of the interpreters for the first time.

So, now it was off to Novgorod, a city of a quarter of a million people. This would be their missionary field for the next two weeks.

The farmers were put up in a hotel that was owned by the Mafia. In the past, other hotels had been tried only to have terrible results such as burglaries and muggings. The missionary fellow figured the Mafia would not shoot up their own hotel, so it might be the safest place. He was right.

For the next two weeks, the farmers would go out each day to meet with people from the struggling Christian church and local farmers.

One thing the farmers had been asked to bring, was garden seeds. They discovered that Russian people are great gardeners, but they do not always have access to seeds.

Dewey's wife was asked to talk about the abortion issue at the Christian Church they were working with. After the service, people just ran up to them to get the "Precious Feet" pins they were giving out. Many were weeping. Some of them had been forced by the government to have abortions even though they did not want to do it.

After the service, his wife found out that she was the first woman to ever speak from the pulpit of the Church. It had never been allowed. She was thankful she had not known that when she went up front to speak. That was an overwhelming experience.

The farmers went out into the bush country to visit with both individual farmers and a government farm. It was shocking how archaic their operations were. Their operations reminded the farmers of what farming was like in the thirty's and forty's in America.

They also discovered that the Russian farmers were stubborn about doing things differently. The Americans realized that their job was not to change farming ways in Russia; it was to give support, encouragement, and share the love of Jesus.

One of the other projects they were involved in was at one of the orphanages. The farmers were asked to dismantle a building on the orphanage grounds.

At first, they thought this would be fairly easy. As they got going, they soon discovered they were actually taking down two buildings in one. One building had just been built over the other one. They were also commissioned to save all the building materials, so this became much more tedious.

During this project, one of the farmers fell through the roof and got hurt. Since no ice was available, Dewey's wife put a frozen fish on his arm to take down the swelling.

Another thing that made this project more difficult was that Dewey was still recovering from a bout with food poisoning. They had gone to a restaurant and the meat he had eaten must not have been cooked properly.

The missionary fellow and Dewey's wife went shopping to pick up some items for lunch. They were especially looking for a couple of bottles of 7-UP. They went to five stores and came up with only one bottle.

They all discovered that the "real" people of Russia are wonderful and delightful people when you have earned their trust. They were still reeling from being under Communism for ninety years. The missionary family had been there long enough that they had earned the trust of the people. That meant that the farmers inherited that trust by being with the missionary family. In spite of their poverty, the Russian people will give until it hurts to show that they appreciate you.

The farmers had the opportunity to eat in the homes of several people. They were fantastic cooks and they never got sick from anything these ladies made.

Every minute was not taken up with work. They were able to tour the countryside, visit Churches, and go shopping.

The time came for the farmers to go home. They had made many Russian friends and leaving them was difficult.

On the way to St. Petersburg, they stopped at St. Peter's castle. This was like a whole park. The missionary fellow had arranged for this and he kept everyone's tickets.

Dewey and his wife got separated from the group. As they roamed the park, they ended up down by the pier when a hydrofoil boat from Finland arrived. It was on the shores of the Baltic Sea.

To get a better look, they started down the pier. When the people disembarked, a lady guard was shouting and pointing for the people to go down the other side of the pier.

When Dewey and his wife turned around to go back from where they came, she yelled for them to go the same way the others were going. As they were walking with the people, it dawned on them that these people were entering the park and were paying for their tickets.

They had no tickets, no proof they came from the park, and could not speak Russian. What to do!!

They did not want to pay again and there was no way they could get the police to believe them. They had to act and do it quickly.

They jumped the fence and ran back through the turn stiles as fast as they could. Behind them, they could hear the police yelling.

"Shtope Shtope, Shtope!!" That was what "stop" sounded like in Russian.

"RUN!!" They had to get where other people were and try to get lost in the crowd.

Finally, they got to a crowd of people and joined them. The police had not caught them. They were exhausted but very grateful.

As they tried to find their way back to their group, they came upon a Finnish restaurant. When they went in, they were shocked at the beauty and precision of the construction. Everything fit together perfectly – unlike Russian construction.

They noticed the restrooms and went in. They were awesome. They were pretty, smelled great, and they did not have to pay for toilet paper. It was also air conditioned.

His wife remained in there for what seemed like an extraordinary amount of time. Finally she came out. She expected to find Dewey waiting for her in the little patio café area, but he was not there. As she sat there, she worried that he came out ahead of her and had been caught by the police.

Finally, he came out of the restroom. He had experienced the same thing she had and also wanted to make it last as long as possible. The air conditioning was great on a hot day, especially after running away from the Russian police.

When the group was back together, it was time to head to St. Petersburg. Here they did some touring of the Hermitage and other city sights. The next morning they headed for home.

When Dewey and his wife returned home, they were eager to share their experience in Russia with others. They were invited to several area churches. His wife brought their photo albums and souvenirs to her school to share with her students. Dewey also spoke at the Kiwanis Club.

It had been a great experience. After that they were so grateful for the freedoms and abundance that they found in America.

Time went on and about two years later, in 1997, the ladies decided they should go back to Russia and do something special for the Russian ladies. Up to this time, all of the trips had focused on the men.

His wife was granted a short leave from her school, and in April the ladies headed back to Russia. Because the ladies did not have their husbands with them, they did not feel comfortable flying into the Moscow Airport.

Going through customs with a fellow from Russia was fine, but they would not have any help. So, they flew into Frankfurt, Germany and took a flight straight to St. Petersburg.

When Satan Came to Moose Lake

In preparing for the trip, the ladies had included in their cargo bags chocolate brownie mix, candy, and bottles of morphine pills for a lady who was dying of bone cancer. She did not have access to any pain medications in Russia and this was going to be a very painful death. The missionary lady's doctor had written the prescriptions and the ladies were the carriers.

Both the chocolate and the morphine were contraband. They could end up in a Russian jail for what they were carrying. They knew they were doing God's will, because each one of them had a peace about the trip beyond anything they could imagine. They soon found out how God was going to take care of the situation.

The plane took off from Frankfurt and for the first thirty minutes everything seemed very normal. Suddenly, the announcement came that they were flying back to Frankfurt due to engine problems. That did not sound good.

When they landed, the passengers had to wait on the plane while the mechanics tried to fix the problem. The Russian and German passengers paced the aisle, talking very loudly. They were very upset about the delay.

The ladies, on the other hand, calmly left the three adjoining seats they had. They took their blankets and moved to some of the unoccupied seats and enjoyed a nap. They knew by that time that God had everything under control; they just had to watch Him work.

The mechanics discovered they could not figure out what the problem was. For safety sake, all the passengers were moved to a different plane and they took off again. This time they made it to St. Petersburg.

In St. Petersburg, the ladies discovered that their delay caused them to arrive at exactly the same time as two other full flights. They found themselves at the end of these very long lines of passengers.

By the time they made their way to the customs booth, the officers could not have cared less if the ladies were eating the brownies from their bags and wearing the morphine around their necks. These people were exhausted. The ladies had made it through the first hurdle. The x-ray station was next.

This was the scariest part. Those machines showed everything. The wife of the FCFI director went through first. She made it. She was not even asked any questions.

Dewey's wife was next. The only thing she was asked was why she was coming to Russia. The answer of course, was to visit friends. So she was passed through. As she waited for the missionary lady to go through, she watched the monitor for the x-ray machine.

Oh, NO!! There was the bottle of morphine pills front and center of her cargo bag. It was right next to the coffee can with bean seeds. She thought they were in BIG TROUBLE.

After scanning the bag, the officer looked at the missionary wife and asked her one question. (Here it comes – they are getting our beds ready for us in the jail right now!) "What is in the large round can?"

"Those are bean seeds for a friend of mine. She cannot afford seeds." she said.

"OK."

They had made it. The minister from the Church ran over and helped the ladies with their bags. They were off to Novgorod.

They knew that God had arranged for them to come in at just the right time and had closed the eyes of the man at the x-ray machine. God be praised!

The ladies were there for ten days. They met with many of their friends.

The ladies went to visit a couple of local schools. Here they shared Bible stories and gave out some seeds. The kids were thrilled.

In one of the high schools, they held a Bible study. Each student was able to use one of the classroom Bibles. As they read and talked in English, it was translated into Russian.

One of the high school teachers asked if they could talk about birth control. Teen pregnancy was a major problem in Novgorod. Being a teacher, Dewey's wife felt the most comfortable discussing this subject.

She shared that the unborn was a real person. She offered the kids "Precious Feet" pins. The kids flocked up to her to get these pins. She also gave them information about adoption as a solution instead of abortion.

The main focus of the trip was the ladies of the Christian Church in Novgorod. They planned to have a special luncheon for ladies only. The minister's wife told them that they could only expect about fifty ladies because it was going to be held Easter weekend and the ladies would have too much to do.

With that in mind, they cooked, set up tables, and decorated for the fifty ladies they expected to come to the garage where the evening service was usually held.

When it came time for the ladies of the Church to come, they just kept on coming. It was awesome. In total, they served ninety-three ladies an American luncheon.

The Americans had only prepared for fifty, but ninety-three showed up! The Russian ladies immediately saw the problem and started sharing cups, plates, silverware, and chairs to make it work.

A few of the men were very suspicious about what was going on. Dewey's wife thought perhaps the men were a bit jealous. The men stayed long enough to have a cup of coffee and make sure everything was O.K. with them.

A wonderful time of fellowship and Bible study was had with the ladies. They had two interpreters to help with language barriers.

When Dewey's wife met her friend with the bone cancer, there was no need for an interpreter. Their spirits united as they held each other, smiled, and each prayed in their own language. That lady is now waiting in heaven, what a joyous reunion that will be!

Shortly after the day of the luncheon, it was time for the ladies to go back home. Through tearful eyes, they bid farewell knowing that most likely the next time they met, it would be in heaven.

The trip home was very uneventful. This was fine as the ladies had experienced quite enough excitement for one trip.

When Dewey's wife came home, she put the wheels in motion for one of the Russian girls to come to America the next summer as part of a 4-H project. She had no idea what next summer would bring.

Just as Dewey and his wife had been asked to tell about their trip together to Russia, so was his wife. The Moose Lake Kiwanis asked her to come to one of their luncheons to share her trip with the businessmen of the community.

She got to the café and began setting up some of her souvenirs for her presentation. Soon the businessmen began arriving. She knew most of them.

Then, a woman came in. She was informed that this was the new Superintendent of the Moose Lake School. His wife could not believe her eyes. This was the most unprofessional looking and acting person she had ever met. During the lunch time, the Superintendent talked in a very loud, boisterous way, sort of what one would expect at a bar.

When lunch was over, it was time for her to give her presentation about Russia. She was introduced and away she went.

Everything went quite well for a while. But when she started sharing about being in the Russian schools, she was distracted by the actions of the Superintendent.

She noticed that the more she talked about Russian schools, reading the Bible, praying, and compared that to the way God was not allowed in American schools, the woman glared viciously at her and squirmed noticeably in her chair.

Dewey's wife was very uncomfortable in front of this woman and moved closer to their family's minister until she was finally standing right next to him. She whispered to him, "PRAY FOR ME!"

She finished her presentation. The businessmen all came over and thanked her. Those that had time asked a few questions. However, the Superintendent had bolted out of the café like a bat out of "you know where" as soon as the presentation was over.

They realized that it was at that moment that the Superintendent had figured out what Dewey was all about. He was an active, Bible believing Christian and she did not like that.

One of Dewey's bus parents told him some time later, that when she was planning the community Vacation Bible School, which was always held at the School, she met with the Superintendent to inform her of this.

The Superintendent had responded by stating that "she prided herself in keeping God out of the School and had no intention of changing that now."

The cloud was black and getting bigger by the minute. The whole community was in trouble and nobody even knew it.

- 22 -

FARMING FOR THE FUTURE

Dewey's life now consisted of raising his family, driving school bus, and farming their two hundred and twenty acre beef farm. It kept him busy, but it was very rewarding.

He had started his beef farm with about twenty-five head of Black Angus calves. Through many years of breeding, he had built up his herd to nearly one hundred and fifty head. They were all in great shape. He enjoyed his animals.

The farm had been worked over the years and the number of productive acres had been raised considerably. He now had over one hundred and twenty-five acres that produced hay, corn, or oats. He also rented hay land.

All through his adult years, Dewey had been open to new ideas in farming. He felt that doing a job the same way year after year simply because that was the way it had always been done was fine, if that was absolutely the only way it could be done. However, he was not afraid to try different ways to get a job done.

It was spring of 1998 and plans were being made on his farm for a public tour of Biosolids spreading. Biosolids were treated sewage sludge partially dried and mixed with lime to make a real good fertilizer.

The plant was located in Duluth, Minnesota. From there it was trucked to qualifying farms. Dewey's was the first farm chosen in the Moose Lake Township.

The Western Lake Superior Sanitary District (WLSSD), along with the Minnesota Pollution Control Agency (MPCA), wanted to have field trials on his farm to show the public that this was a good program for the land.

There had been a lot of opposition to spreading Biosolids by many organizations and individuals. Having a tour like this would give the people a chance to observe the process and watch the results as the new crop grew.

The University of Minnesota set up a tent on one of the fields. There would be coffee, juice, and rolls served. The public would have the opportunity to come and ask questions. The University also sent out over two hundred invitations to government officials, mayors, council members, town boards, and civic organizations.

The day before the tour, all the bus drivers were invited out to the farm for lunch.

The word got out and Dewey was confronted by a neighboring farmer. He stated emphatically that Biosolids would never be put on his farm, even over his dead body.

The big concern about it was the lead content. But every semi load had a computer printout of all nutrients in the load. Dewey had around two hundred semi loads spread over one hundred acres.

The printout showed it contained magnesium, selenium, zinc, and a few other trace elements most people buy over the counter in pill form. People bought these to stay healthy because their fruits and vegetables were lacking these nutrients.

These nutrients had not been reintroduced into the ground after years and years of taking crops off. The ground was depleted of its nutrients and that was why the fruits and vegetables had such a dead taste.

The printout showed that the amount of lead was so negligible; it barely showed up on a semi load.

The night before the field trial, the University asked Dewey for a short meeting at about 7:30 a.m. Dewey asked if they could wait until 8:30 because he had his school bus route to do and that was when he was finished at the bus garage.

These were the "higher ups" in the University system and they had to be in Duluth for a meeting. But they would wait until 8:30.

The morning of the tour, Dewey did his route. He was in a hurry to get back to the farm for his meeting with the University people.

All of a sudden there was a so called "RANDOM" drug test that had to be made. Dewey and three others had to give a urine test. He asked the Supervisor if he could get to a quick meeting with the University people and be back in about half an hour.

The Supervisor, who was a close friend, neighbor, and fellow farmer said,"You leave now and you will be fired!"

Dewey was shocked, to say the least. He wondered why his friend had such an attitude.

The mechanics garage was an unlawful place to have drug tests done because there was no privacy. A person had to carry his specimen in front of everyone. There was always some kind of snickering because they had to do this. There were women that had to take the test also.

Prior to the arrival of Superintendent Moldy, these drugs tests were administered legally at the local clinic. The tests were done at the clinic due to concerns over data privacy issues.

So waiting his turn, he paced back and forth in the repair bay talking to himself about how he was going to get to the meeting on time.

Finally, it was his turn. He went in the tiny toilet area that had a four foot high door and filled the cup.

He stepped out and one of the guys said, "Don't trip, Dewey!"

He responded with, "What you see is what you get."

It was a joke. Like if a person came out of a kitchen with a cup, he might have a cup of orange juice. But if you came out of the bathroom, most likely you wouldn't be carrying orange juice. So don't make a mistake.

The guy giving the test worked for a drug testing company and some schools hired the company to take care of these tests.

Dewey's sample was poured into two vials, filling both of them. The rest was thrown away. Dewey signed the papers and got his copy. He left to get to the meeting.

But, alas, he was too late. The University guys had to get to their meeting in Duluth.

It was a beautiful day for people to come out to watch the spreading of Biosolids. They could see the equipment at work. They were able to get their questions answered and find out the truth about Biosolids. The people received a lot of information that day. About two hundred people attended the tour.

Dewey could tell the tension was building against him for many weeks for putting Biosolids on his fields. Some people made up their minds from stories in other parts of the country. They refused to hear both sides of the story.

Remember, this practice was approved by the MPCA, the most stringent environmental organization in the world. They even sent an official from St. Paul to inspect field operations. They interviewed the applicator to be sure he knew what he was doing.

This inspector was dressed in high heels and walked a long way across the plowed field to get to the operations. Dewey was impressed with her dedication.

Well, the day continued on. People came and asked questions and had lunch. When it came time for his afternoon route, he drove as usual. By the time he came home, everything was all packed up and the tour was over. All that was left to do now was to disk and plant the oats and alfalfa.

That evening, after the show, another farmer friend walked all the way across the plowed field on crutches to where Dewey was disking. He told him how disappointed he was to see Dewey was having Biosolids spread. Dewey had not realized there would be so much opposition to his having Biosolids spread on his farm.

Dewey thought the day had just been one of many exciting days on the farm. He had no idea what was going on behind the scenes. He had no idea that Bart, the bus mechanic, was dead set against the spreading of Biosolids. He did not have a clue that this day would set the stage for the toughest battle of his life to begin in three weeks.

The black cloud was getting bigger and blacker. May God be with him!

- 23 -

THE BLACK CLOUD STRIKES IN 1998

May 14, 1998 started just like every other day had for the last school year. He got to the bus garage at the regular time, chatted with the other drivers, and set out to do his morning route.

After his morning route, the Supervisor came up to Dewey and gave him an envelope. By the way the Supervisor, Bart, had only been working for the District for only a few months.

Dewey opened the envelope and read, "suspension without pay!" It went on to say the following:

> "The purpose of this letter was to inform you that you are hereby suspended without pay, effective immediately.
>
> The grounds for this suspension are that on or about April 23, 1998, you refused to provide an adequate urine sample pursuant to a request that you

participate in a controlled substance test based upon random selection.

Regulations promulgated by the United States Department of Transportation provide, in relevant part as follows:

No driver shall refuse to submit to a ...random alcohol or controlled substance test required under Sec. 382.305, ...No employer shall permit a driver who refuses to submit to such tests to perform or continue to perform safety- sensitive functions.

49 C.F.R. 382.211

Further, federal regulations provide that refusal to provide an adequate urine sample constitutes a refusal to submit to testing, which is deemed to mean that the driver would have tested positive. Federal regulations provide that a driver who tests positive must meet with a substance abuse counselor and submit to further testing. The School District will provide the name of a certified substance abuse counselor to you.

You are hereby directed to contact the substance abuse counselor and arrange to meet with the counselor as soon as possible. You are further directed to cooperate in all respects with the requests of the substance abuse counselor, including any request for additional alcohol or drug testing.

Upon receipt of a full report from the substance abuse counselor, a decision relating to your further employment by the School District will be made."

Sincerely,
Dr. Moldy
Superintendent

Dewey said to his Supervisor, "It looks like you don't want me around here any more." Bart laughed at him and walked away.

He went home and called his wife. She came home from work early. They decided there must have been a mistake.

He had taken more than his share of those tests. Never in his life had he taken any drugs other than Excedrin for a headache once in a while. He never had a drink. He thought for sure his test must have gotten mixed up with someone else.

Dewey's friend, Harold, came over in the afternoon to see what was going on. He was the senior driver. He had only one more year of driving than Dewey.

He showed Harold the suspension letter. He couldn't believe it. Harold said that he was three feet away from the tester. He watched the tester pour Dewey's sample. Dewey wondered if the tester had forgotten to send it in.

Harold was a good honest man. Dewey's family thought the world of him. They had a lot of good times together.

His friend told him to get a copy of the drug test results from the School. He said he had asked Bart a couple weeks before this how the drug testing had gone. Bart told him that everyone passed.

Harold said he did not even know why he would have asked about the test results. There was no one to be suspicious of. Whatever the reason, it really made Dewey suspicious about his test results and the accusation against him.

Dewey was about to find out that he was right to be suspicious, but not in the way he thought. Fear and frustration were moving in. If he had been able to see the black cloud, he would have been shocked at how large and black it was now!

- 24 -

RAWEANA

Dewey had never been a person to just sit back and let things happen to him. He needed to get to the bottom of this accusation and do it fast. There was no way he had tested positive for drugs and he did not want anyone to think he had, especially the bus kids and their families.

The next morning he went out to the bus garage to see his "good friend", Bart. He wanted to see what was going on.

He went out there when the other drivers would be on the route. As he entered the bus garage he called out, "Bart, are you here?"

The heater fan was running and it was pretty noisy. He was looking for Bart but around the corner came Raweana.

Raweana was one of his wife's good friends from school. They both graduated from the Moose Lake School the same year.

Their families had been good friends for many years. Raweana's husband was also one of his wife's classmates.

Raweana and her family had experienced a devastating fire. It completely burned down their home. They lost nearly all of their personal belongings.

As soon as Dewey heard about this, he and his wife went out to Raweana's place. They offered them a place to stay with their children and anything else they might need.

At that time, Dewey was a deacon at his Church. He went to the Deacon Board on behalf of Raweana and her family to ask for assistance. The Deacons had what was called a "Benevolence Fund." that could be used to help people in the community.

Their family never went to a church. The Deacons decided to help Raweana and her family even though they had no connection to the Church. It would be a good way to show that they cared. Dewey brought a check out to them on behalf of the Church to help with their immediate needs.

The ladies group of the Church sponsored a shower for Raweana and her family. They received many new or slightly used items they needed in their home when they rebuilt.

Dewey was close to both Raweana and her husbands' parents. They were all good honest farming people.

Raweana's father-in-law developed cancer. She was the one to bring him to the doctor. One day, she came to work very distraught over his condition. She was very upset and crying. Dewey was always the one she came to for comfort. She talked to him everyday because Dewey knew her father-in-law and cared about him. They always ended in a hug.

He asked Raweana where Bart was.

"Well, he had to do a route for someone who was sick because there isn't enough subs".

Dewey told Raweana, "I don't know what is going on, so I came to talk to Bart about it." He also said he sure would appreciate it if the bus drivers would support him.

Oh boy, did she get mad! "Why should we help you when nobody came to help me when I was suspended?!"

Raweana had always been a very emotional person. It took nothing for her to start crying.

By this time, she was babbling words of hate for one of the other female bus drivers that was considered cute, sexy and flirted her way out of any jam she got into.

This other driver would call Bart "Sweetheart", and say "Bye honey" when she went to her bus. That was not good. Bart was married and in the past had many relationships with other women.

Raweana was a husky farm wife. She was about three inches taller than Dewey. She was a hard working farm wife.

Raweana had an awfully hard time driving bus, especially in the winter. They called the wrecker many times because she misjudged the ditch. Also, on extra curricular trips, she would drive over curbs, hit highway signs, and lose control. The kids would get scared.

In the parking lot at a school on the Iron Range, she backed into a car and wrecked the hood. Raweana got scared and left the scene of her accident.

The people she hit followed her all the way to Moose Lake and filed a claim against the School.

On a trip with the football team she was hauling through Duluth, she hit a light pole trying to go around it.

There were five women bus drivers and no matter what they did, nothing was ever done discipline wise. One of the ladies backed into a power pole. It broke off and landed on the top of the bus. It burnt a hole all the way through two layers of metal. Sparks were flying all over near the kids who were in the bus.

She had no idea what to do and frantically called on the radio for help. One of the male drivers, who was later fired, told her to "drive out from under the pole." They all wondered what kind of trouble she would get into for this accident. She bragged later that she did not even have to go see the Superintendent.

While talking to Dewey that morning, Raweana brought up an accident she was involved in. One day, Raweana and "the flirt" had a trip to Duluth, to the University of Minnesota. On the way back, they were racing up Thompson Hill. This was a long steep grade with a truck lane and two other lanes.

One bus had more power and one driver thought she was ahead far enough and swung in front of the other.

This caused a very bad accident. Miraculously, no one got hurt. The police investigated and made their report.

After this accident, there were many parent complaints. The School had to give a suspension to someone, so they suspended Raweana. They would never say for how long or put anything in writing.

So Raweana sat at home while "the flirt" was just as sassy as ever and still driving her route with no consequence at all.

In telling Dewey how unfair she was treated, she of course broke down in tears. Being that they had been friends for many years, they hugged until she settled down. Then she went on her route and Dewey went home.

He went back out to the bus garage about eleven o'clock a.m. to see Bart. Boy, he was mad at Dewey for hurting Raweana. Bart said Dewey should apologize to her.

He asked Bart, "What in the world do you think I did to her?"

"You hurt her."

Dewey went out to Raweana's farm to talk. Her husband met him outside on the steps. He asked if Raweana was around.

"She don't want to talk to you."

"Why?" Dewey asked.

Raweans's husband just shrugged his shoulders.

Dewey started to tell him what happened. Raweana came out but she would not speak. He told his thoughts and apologized for no one taking an interest when she was suspended for the accident with "the flirt".

He said he was sorry she had hard feelings against him. Raweana would not say a word to him.

She would not, and has not forgiven him to this day. She has let herself be consumed by hate.

Dewey left for the bus garage to see Bart. He asked for a copy of the drug test result. Bart said, "We don't have it."

"Where is it?"

"I don't know."

"Can you get it for me?"

Bart was getting so fidgety now, that Dewey was really getting even more suspicious of him.

So he went home and had his wife type a letter to the Superintendent asking for his test results.

In the meantime, Bart was busy telling every body at Art's Café that Dewey had failed a drug test.

Harold revealed that Bart had told him about the suspension before Dewey was even given his suspension letter. That was breaking the Minnesota and Federal laws on confidentiality.

Bart was defaming Dewey's name all over town to ruin his reputation all over the state. Dewey later discovered he would not be able to get a job in Minnesota again.

The following day, he again went to the bus garage to see Bart.

"Do you have the information for me?"

Bart gave him an envelope and told him in no uncertain terms "Don't you come out here again!"

Dewey got in the car and went home to read the letter. It said, "You are hereby ordered not to come on school property and hand in all your keys." Wow! Things were now going from bad to worse. Constantly on his mind was "What on earth is going on?"

Then he found out that Raweana had filed charges against him with the School. In her charges, she claimed that Dewey scared her.

That was more than a little hard to imagine. Raweana was a big farm girl. In fact, for fun one day at the bus garage, she got him in a head lock and said, "I can take you any time."

Prior to this day, Raweana had come to do her afternoon route very tired. The drivers always got there ten minutes before leaving for the school, which was two miles away.

"What's the matter Raweana?"

"I was combining oats and the axle broke so I jacked the machine up and took out the broken pieces. We had an old junker combine for parts. So I got the axel from it but I didn't have time to get it put together. I had to get here. I've gotta get the combining done before it rains."

The drivers were all very impressed. Dewey had known Raweana all his life so it didn't surprise him.

Knowing how strong Raweana was, Dewey could not believe that she was trying to convince anyone that he had scared her or hurt her in anyway. Anyone who actually thought about the two of them should have realized how truly ridiculous that was.

At this point Bart refused to communicate anything and Dewey was not allowed to talk to the Superintendent or the School Board because of a chain of command policy. This was much like the Army, which he was used to.

He called Bart and asked where the School wanted him to go to get the drug counseling. Dewey said, "I want to get this cleared up before the end of the school year so my bus kids can get there annual picnic."

- 25 -

DRUG TEST RESULTS

Dewey had asked Bart for his drug test results several times. Bart was very nervous, vague, and would never respond to his question. Then Dewey wrote a letter to the School requesting a copy of his drug test results. All he received had been orders to not come on School property. No test results came.

By this time, several days had passed. He had a very sinking, suspicious feeling that something was very, very wrong.

Bart had told Harold that everyone had passed the tests, but the School was now saying Dewey tested positive which meant that he had failed the test. That did not make any sense at all.

He and his wife decided that if the School would not give him his test results, perhaps the drug testing company would.

Dewey contacted the company from Coleraine, Minnesota that collected the testing samples. When he spoke to the receptionist about finding out about his test, she asked if anyone from the testing lab in Chicago had contacted him. The answer was "no".

She said, "If no one from the lab contacted you by phone, you tested negative."

She then went on to explain that the lab only contacted a drug sample donor if the test was positive. In fact, the donor would be contacted before the employer, in case there were extenuating circumstances such as being on a special medication or eating poppy seeds that might trigger a false positive.

She told him to wait while she found his folder. Moments later when she came back on the phone, she was rather upset.

Dewey's folder had been right on her desk the day before. Now she could not find it. She went to the filing cabinet to see if it was there.

Now she was really confused. She could not imagine where his folder would be. As she thought about this, she remembered that the previous day, the Superintendent from Moose Lake had been to the facility. She thought that was odd also. She asked Dewey to wait a moment while she went to ask her boss about this.

When she came back, she suddenly went from being very helpful to reluctant to continue the conversation and ended it.

In hind sight, it was obvious that she had just been told by her boss not to give out anymore information or talk to Dewey anymore.

The next day, Dewey called that facility again. He asked for the phone number for the testing lab in Chicago. She gave that information and hung up.

Dewey contacted the testing lab. This was the first time he had ever had to do anything like this. In the past he had never had to worry about what anyone did with his sample because the results were always negative.

Finally he got through to the correct person at the testing lab. He gave them his name, Social Security Number, and the testing number on his form.

After a few moments of checking their records, the lady told him that he had passed with no problems.

He told her that the School told him he had flunked. The lady's immediate response was that they could not do that and that he better get an attorney.

She said that the testing lab was the only one who could determine if someone passed or failed a test. She also promised that the company would testify on his behalf.

Now that he knew for sure that he had passed the drug test, he needed proof in writing. He asked how he could get a copy of his test results.

He was surprised to find out how simple it would be. All he had to do was write a letter containing the same information he had given her and include a check for ten dollars. As soon as they received it, they would send him the results.

In the meantime, Dewey got an attorney from Wisconsin. He petitioned the court stating that Dewey had a right to his own drug test results.

The School had said they were the only ones who had the right to it. They refused to give him a copy of his own drug test, even though State and Federal laws stated clearly that the donor was the owner of the test results.

In the court battle the School lost. They even appealed their case stating that Dewey had no right to see his drug report.

Because the School had appealed, they still did not give him his test results. Going through the court system would take months.

Dewey was very glad he had taken matters into his own hands. Just a few days later, he received a copy of his drug test results from the laboratory in Chicago.

There it was in black and white. He had been tested for five substances. There was not a trace of anything in his sample. He tested completely negative. THE MOOSE LAKE SCHOOL WAS LYING! He wondered why they would go to such extravagant lengths.

Then he thought back to his friend, Allen. He began to put a few pieces together. He was a Christian and the Superintendent did not like that.

- 26 -

GOING TO DRUG COUNSELING

The School must have thought that if they made an accusation, it would not be challenged. That was what happened with most people. They were afraid of more repercussions, so they just quietly backed off and accepted whatever was said or done.

Now the School had to cover their tracks. They did not want to be caught in an embarrassing situation, but the more the Superintendent did, the worse it got.

Dewey knew that the Superintendent's suspension letter stated that he was supposed to go see a drug counselor. The School would then take the results of that assessment and decide if he would be reinstated or not.

Bart took his old sweet time getting this information to Dewey but finally he was told to go to the Phoenix Center in Cloquet. This was a town about twenty miles away.

He did not know at that time that even though she put this all in writing, the Superintendent had no intention of reinstating him no matter what the outcome was.

Dewey set up a meeting with a counselor at the Phoenix Center and brought his wife. Neither of them had experienced anything like this before. They were absolutely dead set against drug or alcohol use, so they found this a very embarrassing and scary experience.

When they got to the Phoenix Center, the first thing the lady told them was not to try to fool her. Between her and her husband, they had over forty years in assessing and curing drug and alcohol problems.

She said, "We have seen it all. Take these tests and answer honestly, because I can tell by your answers if you are lying."

Dewey filled out the questionnaire. The counselor was surprised he got done so fast. She then started the oral questioning.

After several questions, Dewey leaned forward in his chair, looked her in the eye, and said, "You are looking at virgin lips, M'am. The only drugs I have had in my life were Excedrin for a headache once in a while. I don't even drink coffee."

She got up and left the room. She had put his wife in the waiting room to take some tests also. She checked to be sure his wife had finished her questionnaire. Then the two of them went back to her office and Dewey was sent out to the waiting room.

In her office, the counselor looked over the questionnaire briefly. Then she asked a few questions about whether Dewey was taking drugs, how long he had been taking drugs, and if she felt safe with Dewey.

His wife finally had enough with the questioning. She looked at the counselor and emphatically stated that her husband was not doing drugs now and never had done drugs. She then stated that when it came to drugs, her husband had "virgin lips". He never smoked, drank, or did drugs. She stated, "He doesn't even drink coffee."

The counselor called Dewey into her office. She looked at both of them and said, "WHAT ARE YOU DOING HERE?"

Dewey said he really did not know. He was just doing what the Superintendent had told him to do. He told her that the Superintendent said he flunked the drug test.

She asked if he had the drug test result. He informed her that the School had refused to give him a copy of his drug test results. At that time the test results had not arrived from the testing lab yet.

She left the room. When she came back, she said that Bart, Dewey's Supervisor would not talk to her.

She said that with all of her years of counseling people with drug and alcohol problems, she knew when there was a problem with substance abuse and when there was not.

It was obvious to her that Dewey was not doing drugs. She said there was a problem with the Superintendent and Supervisor that needed to be resolved.

The counselor from the Phoenix Center got the report off to the School immediately so Dewey could get reinstated before School was over.

Her written recommendation was to resolve the problem between the Supervisor and Dewey.

It became obvious that the Superintendent was not going to resolve the problem. She made every excuse she could think of to prevent Dewey from being reinstated.

Her next roadblock was to say that Dewey needed a release from his doctor to go back to work. So Dewey went to see the doctor. He told her the problem. She was very understanding. The doctor's office sent a fax to the Superintendent so she would get it in time for Dewey to finish off the end of the year.

The Superintendent would not accept the fax. The doctor's office even phoned her directly. The Superintendent would not accept that either. The only thing the Superintendent would accept was a letter sent by registered mail.

The Superintendent was then conveniently out of the office for a week just before School was out. That meant Dewey didn't get his job back and his kids didn't get their annual picnic.

In the meantime Bart was telling everyone at Arts Café that,"IF DEWEY COMES BACK IN THE FALL I'LL MAKE SURE HE GETS FIRED!"

Can you, the reader, see the black cloud yet?

- 27 -

SNAKES IN THE GRASS

At the very end of the school year, a horrible tragedy hit the little town of Moose Lake. A young girl named Katie was working late at the Subway one night when she was abducted.

Hundreds of people from the area joined the search for her. The bus drivers from Moose Lake, who were available, were called upon to drive the searchers from the staging area to the search areas. They were driving very long shifts. Dewey's friend, Harold, shared with him how exhausted the drivers were getting.

Since this had nothing to do with the School and the drivers were volunteering their time, Dewey thought he could at least help with the search by driving.

So, Dewey went looking for Bart to let him know he was willing to help with the search. He found Bart back behind the Depot in the bus of one of the female drivers.

When Dewey got to the bus both Bart and the female had very guilty looks on their faces. Bart jumped out of the bus so the other driver would not hear the conversation between Dewey and himself.

Dewey informed Bart that he was reinstated and available to help with the driving. Bart just ignored him, jumped in his truck, and sped away.

Why was Bart in that other driver's bus? Why were they parked in an out of the way, obscure area? Why did they have such guilty looks on their faces? And, of course, why wouldn't Bart let him drive for such an important situation as this? These were questions he continues to ponder to this day.

Dewey had lived in the Moose Lake community all of his life. People should have known what he was all about by this time. That did not seem to matter.

All summer the fury mounted against him. Many times he was out in the yard working and people would lean out the windows of their cars and holler obscenities at him. Most of the time, he did not even know who these people were.

Wherever he went people he had known all his life would walk across the street rather than cross his path and meet him.

During the summer, his family received over two hundred obscene phone calls. He contacted the phone company and they could not do anything about it, except to suggest that he change his phone number. When he contacted the Sheriff's department, they couldn't do anything about it either.

In July, 1998 Dewey and his wife went to the fiftieth anniversary open house for a close farmer friend of the family. Bart and his wife were at this party. Here Dewey met some of his relatives from Grand Marais, which is located about three hours north of Moose Lake along Lake Superior.

This should have been a fun and happy event. However, they noticed a distinct coldness among the relatives.

His brother-in-law came over to talk to him and Dewey invited him up to the farm. When his brother-in-law arrived, he wanted to go for a walk with Dewey.

When they were away from the house, his brother-in-law turned to Dewey. He was just shaking he was so angry. He had heard at the party that Dewey was suspended for using drugs and refusing to take a drug test. He was livid. Dewey tried to explain what really happened, but to no avail. He was too angry to listen.

Before the day of this party, Dewey's wife had just finished putting together a file folder that contained copies of his drug test results which had finally arrived.

Dewey brought his brother-in-law back to the house. By this time, his wife had shown the folder to the brother-in-law's wife. So she understood what was really happening.

His brother-in-law looked over the drug test results. He was still a bit skeptical. But he could not argue with what was in black and white. They all sat down together and discussed the matter.

In time, his brother-in-law became a strong ally. They were some of his best prayer partners. They also supported Dewey and his family financially.

It was a shame that so few people were interested in the truth. He carried his folder everywhere he went, just in case someone was interested.

Dewey did everything he could think of to get the matter resolved. Having these false allegations made against him and then not being able to get himself cleared, really took its toll on him both emotionally and psychologically.

He was not able to eat or sleep. Every time there was a noise of any kind, he jumped. The viciousness of the community made him paranoid. He was not able to answer the telephone. When someone came in their driveway, if he did not recognize the vehicle, he would crouch down and hope they would go away. He just could not deal with the harassment. It was more than he could handle.

At night, he could not sleep. He would read his Bible for hours on end. It helped to remind him that God still loved him, but it did not take the fear away. People, who have not gone through a thing like this, just cannot understand how debilitating it becomes.

A few people told him to read the story of Job in the Bible. It took Dewey six months to read this book. He just could not stand the heartache Job went through. It was too close to what he was going through. He finally had to skip to the end of the book to find the good ending. That encouraged him greatly. Perhaps there would be a good ending in a book for him someday.

At the end of July, the Russian girl, that his wife had arranged to come as part of the 4-H program, arrived. Dena (Diana) had just turned fifteen so she was eligible for a passport.

It was still difficult to get out of Russia. They would only let one family member out at a time. They figured if the rest of the family was still in Russia, the person would be sure to come back.

During her visit, Dewey and his wife tried to act as normal as they could. Because he was having such trouble sleeping, he ended up having a pounding headache one day. He sat in the porch with his head in his hands.

Diana found him and sat down on the floor in front of him.

She asked, "Papa, what is wrong?"

He told her he had a headache, but she pressed him to find out why. He told her the School where he drove bus was accusing him of something he had not done.

She then took his hands in hers and prayed about his headache. He could feel the power in that young girl's prayer. Warmth enveloped him and when she finished, his headache was gone.

A day or so later, when they were all seated at the table, Dewey got a phone call he had to take. He did not say anything about it when he sat down. Diana turned to him and said, "That was a bad call, wasn't it?" He answered that indeed, it was.

Diana wanted to pray for him. She really wanted to petition God on his behalf. So, she asked if it would be alright if she prayed in Russian.

That was an awesome prayer. They could sense that her prayer was definitely reaching God's ears. Even though they could not understand what she prayed, they were so blessed and encouraged by having this little Russian girl pray for them with such passion.

By the end of the summer, Dewey felt that he could not safely drive a bus load of kids. He and his wife would be driving to Cloquet, and he would suddenly be lost. He would have no idea where he was and had to ask her where they were and many times where they were going. He was terrified that if he tried to drive a bus load of kids, he would become so distracted by his situation, he would make a mistake that hurt a child. He knew he could not let that happen.

He made an appointment to see a counselor. He thought that would help. He hoped that the counselor would understand the responsibility and safety involved with driving kids.

What he learned was that if a person did not threaten to kill themselves or others, the counselor was not interested in helping. The fact that Dewey could accidentally harm a child through inattentive driving did not seem to matter to him. He was of no help at all.

Through the years, Dewey had developed a very good custom haying business. He had many customers and the summers were always very busy with putting up their hay along with his own. He thought he could still drive the equipment. At least, if anything went wrong, he would be the only one hurt.

When the false accusations made it around the community, not one person called to have haying done. He was out of that business practically over night. His family had always counted on this extra income to help meet their bills.

As the school year approached, Dewey had his lawyer explain his concerns about driving his kids. How could he be behind the wheel of a bus, driving other people's kids, when he could not even make it to Cloquet without help?

Upon the advice of his attorney and for the safety of the kids, Dewey did not appear for the first day of School. The lives of his bus kids were worth more to him than anything the School could possibly do.

Early one evening, the Sheriff came over. Dewey was in the yard and his wife was in the house. She had just gotten home from work. They watched as he drove up the driveway.

All of their boys were away from home. Their hearts just about gave out. The only reason either of them could imagine for a Sheriff to be coming to their place was that something happened to one of their sons.

His wife was about to run outside to see what happened, when their youngest son returned home from football practice. Well, at least he was safe. She wondered what it might be that had befallen one of the other two.

A parent always is concerned about the safety of their children. Parents try to prepare for the worst; one is never really prepared when you find out something bad may have happened.

The Sheriff got out of his vehicle and walked over to where Dewey was standing. He pulled out an envelope and handed it to Dewey.

It was from the Moose Lake School. It demanded that Dewey contact Bart and appear for work on October 6th.

The Superintendent had hired the Sheriff to deliver mail! That was ridiculous. As a parent, she would have known how upsetting it would be to have the Sheriff unexpectedly arrive at their home.

They were to find out that was not going to be her only act of meanness. She would hire the Sheriff to deliver her mail on two more occasions.

Shortly after the Sheriff's visit, the retired Captain of the Northeast Minnesota Police visited Dewey. When the incident with the Sheriff delivering mail was shared with him, he was incensed. He immediately went to the phone to call the Sheriff's department to find out why they were delivering mail.

He discovered that this cost the District seventy-five dollars each time. He was angry. The School claimed to be having financial problems, yet she could afford to hire the Sheriff to deliver mail that could easily have been delivered by the post office. She would use any means of intimidation she could think of, no matter what the cost.

His friend went on to tell about the situation he encountered with Superintendent Moldy. He had an appointment with her to discuss offering a Carnegie Speaking class for her high school students.

He was an instructor of this prestigious program. He was also willing to do the program for free. This was a value of several thousand dollars.

When he arrived for his meeting, the Superintendent was sitting at her desk eating jelly rolls. She was stuffing one in her mouth while the jelly and powdered sugar dripped down her arm and onto her dress.

He could not believe such a lack of professionalism from a Superintendent. He presented his offer to her. She was rude and arrogant. She refused his offer to do this program for the students.

He left and made an appointment with the neighboring School. They welcomed him and his program with open arms.

He still wanted the Moose Lake students to have this opportunity but it had to be done only by word of mouth. Dr. Moldy would not allow this opportunity to be advertised to the students so they could participate.

The reason Dewey's friend had stopped over that day, was to be sure that his youngest son knew about this Carnegie class. He gave Dewey's son a personal invitation to attend.

It turned out that their son and one other student from Moose Lake were the only ones to have this opportunity. It was an awesome opportunity and the students learned a lot about public speaking and how to present themselves in a variety of situations.

What a shame that so few had this advantage. The Superintendent had said no to a wonderful opportunity just because she had the power to do so.

During the summer, it had become obvious to Dewey that his health was in jeopardy from all the stress he was experiencing. He went back to the doctor at the local clinic. She had prescribed some medications and was keeping an eye on his condition.

When Dewey received the order to go back to work, he went back to his doctor for an evaluation. The doctor stated that he was not ready to drive school bus yet.

The Superintendent was not at all happy with this news. She liked to call the shots and her ultimatum was not working.

She was even more unhappy when she was served with the notice that Dewey had filed charges against her and the School in District Court on October 6th.

At first the Union (AFSCME) just stood on the sidelines watching to see" where the chips would fall." Dewey called the state Union office. They told him that if his field representative did not actively represent him, he could be charged with lack of representation.

Finally after pressure of a threat from Dewey to file charges against to the Union for lack of representation, the Union scheduled a meeting with the school. It took four months for the AFSCME Union to get in and give any support.

Due to the restraining order the School had imposed on Dewey, he had to ask in writing and get written permission from the School to come on School property for his own Union meeting.

With the letter in his hand, Dewey, his attorney, and the Union Representative arrived for the scheduled meeting.

Dewey's attorney presented his case. After the meeting with the School Board, the Union Representative came over to Dewey. He shook his hand and stated emphatically that he believed Dewey. The Union would be behind him one hundred percent.

The Union did a lot of negotiating with the School. They finally paid a lawyer from Minneapolis to take his case to conciliation court.

The witnesses were all contacted and paid. They were to meet with the Judge the next day. The School did not want to be humiliated in court with the evidence that was against them so they cut a deal.

Eight hours before the conciliation meeting, the Union lawyer called Dewey to tell him that a deal had been reached and he would get a letter telling him all about it.

He was waiting for a letter to come in the mail or from the Sheriff, but it did not come. A week passed. Dewey decided to call the Union lawyer.

He could not believe that Dewey was not back driving and that he had not gotten a letter from the School explaining the settlement.

Two weeks after that, Dewey got a letter of reprimand from the School.

It stated that if he got a doctor's release, he would be reinstated. That sounded great! He still had a lawsuit pending, but at least he would be back to driving his bus route.

He took a friend of his out to the bus garage. He timed it so they would arrive shortly before the drivers went on the afternoon route. He gave Bart, the Supervisor, his letter from the doctor. Dewey told him the Superintendent already had her letter.

Bart said he knew that and told him to start his old route in the morning. For goodwill, Dewey brought jelly rolls out to the bus garage for everyone.

Three hours later he got a call from Bart saying that he couldn't drive the next day. He told Dewey he didn't know why.

When all of this was going on, his youngest son was a senior at Moose Lake School. His son had a band concert coming up. Again, due to the restraining order, Dewey had to give a written request for permission to come on School grounds so he could attend the concert.

With his permission slip in hand, Dewey and his wife set out for the concert. Just before they entered the building, a guy came right up to Dewey. He put his face right into Dewey's face and said, "No druggy is going to drive my kids to school!"

This was devastating. They had all they could do to compose themselves and go in. They were bound and determined not to let Dewey's situation ruin their son's last year of school.

They went up to the balcony to sit. The whole auditorium was crowded. When they sat down about twenty people around them got up and walked out. Obviously, the rumor mill that Bart started had made its way to the whole community.

Their son was captain of the football team that year. They did not have to ask permission to go to the home games because they were played on the field of a cooperating District. When they attended the games, they had to be sure they stood with the families of the neighboring School so they could avoid harassment.

Time after time, when they wanted to attend their son's senior year activities, Dewey had to write to get permission to go on School property. This was embarrassing and humiliating.

He was the only person to ever be banned from coming on School property. Even the parent who arrived at the School drunk and screaming at everyone, was not banned from the property.

At the end of January, Dewey and his attorney decided that asking permission to go on School property was ridiculous and demeaning.

Dewey wrote a letter to the School stating that he was no longer going to be writing for permission to attend his son's activities.

The Superintendent responded with a letter stating that since he had been reinstated, there was no need for him to ask for permission. When was he reinstated? He and his lawyer figured it must have been following the "deal" with the Union.

The next question was, "If he was reinstated in September or October, why did she accept and give permission three more times and not say anything?" This was another example of her ways of controlling and intimidating her employees.

In May, the National Honor Society had their induction ceremony and awards. The whole National Honor Society of Moose Lake voted to give his son a special award.

His son was to be seated in the audience and be called up on stage at a special time in the ceremony.

His son was a much respected young man by his peers. As stated before, he was captain of the football team. He was an excellent trombone player and he had a really fun sense of humor.

First, they had the induction of the new Honor Society members. As each one came forward, the Superintendent shook their hands and they sat back down.

Finally it was time for his son's award. He was called up on stage by the band director, who was also the advisor of the Honor Society. When he got to the stage, Dr. Moldy turned on her heel and would not acknowledge him. She sat down and left him to stand on stage in embarrassment.

Thankfully, the advisor saw what was happening, and jumped up from his seat to shake his hand and motion for him to be seated with the other members of the Honor Society.

The Superintendent took her hatred for Dewey and put it on an innocent young man. They found out she had done this all her life. She was an abuser of power. She was a woman who had been teased mercilessly all through her life about her obesity. Her goal in life was to get back at any one she could. She was the typical scorned woman.

The family wondered what the Superintendent would do on graduation day. She was up on stage with the chairman of the School Board. The chairman handed out diplomas and she shook each graduate's hand.

When it was his son's turn, he walked right up to her. She turned her head to ignore him. He just stood there with his hand extended, holding up the line until she acknowledged him. She was getting nervous about how this was looking. She was forced to do something. Finally, she had to shake his hand. Pitiful, simply pitiful!

He said afterwards that he wanted to give her a very "firm" handshake.

The Superintendent was not the only one that did despicable things. Numerous times, people knocked his mail box down. One time he found it about a quarter of a mile away in the ditch. To solve this problem, he put up a new mailbox attached to a railroad tie sunk about four feet into the ground. This ended the mailbox ordeal.

Remember, Dewey raised beef cattle on their farm. One day somebody hooked their truck to a gate and ripped it out. All of his cattle got out. Of course, they did a lot of damage to the neighbors' lawns.

The evildoers knew when he wasn't home. When he returned he could count on the fence wires being cut. Then he would have to get his son out of School to help him get the animals back in. Since they lived so close to town, the one hundred and thirty-four head of cattle usually headed for town.

It became obvious after a period of time that he would have to sell the cattle. It had taken forty years of breeding and care to develop one of the finest herds in the county.

The buyers at the sales barn knew as soon as they saw his cattle in the ring that they were of the finest quality. His cattle brought the highest price when he brought them there in the fall of 1999.

He brought them all the way to southern Minnesota to get away from the animosity of potential buyers in his own area. Even local truckers refused to haul for him.

What that Superintendent and Bart did that fateful day in May, 1998 started a six year court battle that Dewey would not give up for anything.

A hearing was scheduled for July 1st that summer. He went before a settlement judge in Duluth, Minnesota. Judge Erogance was the most arrogant person you could ever expect to meet.

Dewey did not know when he went to court, that on that day the Duluth News Tribune had run a story about his case.

During the hearing, he found out there was a statement in the paper stating that he had called someone a "Commie". That was a lie. He had just been to Russia. He had several friends there and would never call anyone a "Commie".

The Judge read the newspaper and made his determination on the case from the newspaper account.

It was at the hearing that Dewey found out all he needed to know about his own attorney. His lawyer could not talk. He had no idea what evidence was and could not answer simple questions the Judge asked him.

He was asked, "What did Bart do?" Half of the case had to do with the fact that Bart spread false rumors and federally protected information about Dewey and his drug test and other things to the public. They had documented proof from many witnesses.

The Judge looked at Dewey and threatened all kinds of things. He stated, "If your case goes to trial, you will lose. There has never been a jury case in Northeast Minnesota that has won a civil case."

Dewey would not give in to the Judge's intimidation. He felt the only way to vindicate himself was to have a jury trial. He needed his good reputation back.

Some of his bus route kids came with a parent to see what happens in a court. After the hearing, the kids and their mother came to Dewey's house to discuss what had happened.

The 6th grade boy said "I thought judges were supposed to be impartial." What could one say, when a twelve year old boy understood better than the judge what a judge's job was supposed to be?

The family found that the wheels of "injustice" roll ever so slowly. It certainly did not help that his attorney could not get things filed with the court on time. This would set everything back many months.

They had been advised that the case would not actually go to court for another three to five years. That was a long time off.

Dewey felt that with Bart's threat to get him fired and the way the Superintendent stalled when he tried to get back to driving, that it would not be safe for him to drive until the lawsuit was completed. He had a very strong feeling that he would be set up for other negative events.

He was concerned that it could involve the students. It would be very easy to "jimmy" the brakes or loosen the lug nuts on the wheels. If these kinds of things were done, it would not be noticed until it was too late. Kids' lives were at stake.

The School had finally granted Dewey a leave of absence for the previous year. His attorney filed a letter petitioning the School to extend this leave until the lawsuit was resolved.

While Dewey could not yet see the black cloud of evil, he could feel it all around him. It was oppressive. He just did not understand yet what was causing all that oppression. But he soon would.

- 28 -

THE GRANT WRITER

During the time that Dewey was waiting for his trial to begin, others from the Moose Lake School District were experiencing the wrath of the Superintendent.

When she was angry at a person, she would scream and yell obscenities at him. Her office was at the end of the elementary wing. She would follow people into the hallway screaming vulgar things at them. The teachers would have to rush to close their doors so their students would not be exposed to the language that came from her mouth.

There were about ten early retirements that year. Teachers would rather take a lower retirement pension than stay on staff and risk what she might do to them.

In addition to the early retirements, there were nearly thirty people pink slipped or fired. These were good, honest teachers. Then the Superintendent called back those teachers that she could manipulate and intimidate. She did not want people on staff who would stand up to her evil tactics.

One of the elementary teachers related to Dewey the situation she found herself in at Moose Lake.

She became interested in grant writing. The Principal and Superintendent said they would hire her to write grants in her spare time.

So she went back to college and got the necessary degrees and knowledge needed to write grants.

She started writing some small grants and was paid by the School District for her work.

Then she was asked to write and apply for some large grants that would total around a hundred and fifty thousand dollars.

She went to the Board and asked for a contract for the job. She wanted to be paid a "per hour" rate for the work she did.

She also needed extra time away from her already over loaded duties as a classroom teacher. She did not get a contract but it was written in the School Board minutes that they would pay her $10.00 an hour for grant writing.

For months, she worked hard on several grants. She worked late at night. She gave up family functions.

One day Superintendent Moldy and the Principal had a big celebration in downtown Moose Lake. They had the mayor, council members, and the county commissioners in attendance. The press was there as well as other dignitaries.

They were announcing the grand opening of the South Polar Learning Center which would house Head Start and other programs.

The A & L TV building had been bought with grant money that was obtained by the Superintendent and Principal. Oh boy, they took all the glory for all the hard work the grant writing lady had done.

When she found out, she was crushed. She asked the Principal why they had done this to her. He had been so helpful to her and she considered him a friend she could depend on.

After this he would avoid her at all cost. He would not answer her questions.

When she wanted to get paid the ten thousand dollars she was due, they all avoided her. She brought the evidence to the School Board. Her name was on the grant as the author. The grant stated that she was the one who was to receive the ten thousand dollars. They promised they would take care of it.

They took care of it by giving her the good old Moose Lake run around. Someone got the ten thousand dollars and it wasn't the grant writer. Who do you think it was that got the money? Hmmmm! Very interesting!

She was then systematically ostracized from the School. For her it was like dying and seeing her life flash before her eyes. It was devastating to be so flagrantly abused.

It took such a toll on her that she could no longer work in this dishonest environment anymore. She resigned. Of course, this was the goal of the School. After they got everything out of a person for free, they just threw them away. So, like many others, she just drifted away to make room for another unsuspecting victim.

- 29 -

MISSOURI

The evil was growing in Moose Lake. There was evil everywhere, but not to the extent that it had permeated this little community.

When the Superintendent arrived, it was as if she brought with her a legion of demons to attack and persecute good people.

The School was not the only area of the community to feel this evil. The prison got a new warden. This woman turned out to be a far left-wing, liberal lesbian. All workers had to adhere to accepting homosexuality or they would pay a price.

She wanted to have a gay pride day at the prison. One of the counselors was a Christian and this went against what the Bible says in Leviticus 18:22, "And you shall not lie with a male as with a woman; it is an abomination."

He did not comply with her wishes, so his office was moved down into the basement of the facility. This was more like a dungeon. But he held his ground because he knew it was the right thing to do.

In the meantime, the community made it impossible to live. Dewey could not get a job of any kind. He applied for a driving job in a neighboring community.

When he went to his interview, the bus supervisor there said in front of the Superintendent, "Why are you here? I heard your bus driving license was revoked." There was no way the Superintendent was going to give him a job after hearing this comment. Dewey never had his license revoked by the state or anyone else. Here was another lie that was going through the community.

Dewey had more support from the community where his wife worked than where he had lived for his whole life. They did not even know him but they knew her as an honest person and that was enough for them.

Her Principal was so kind and understanding. One day she came to work very upset by the condition of Dewey that morning. When her Principal came to see her, he realized right away that something was wrong. When she shared what her concerns were, he immediately instructed her to go home. He took over her classes himself until a substitute could be found.

By this time, the viciousness of the community was spilling over to include his wife. When she met people she knew in the aisle of the grocery store, they would whip their carts around and go to a different aisle.

One day she came down one of the aisles and noticed a mother with her twin sons standing and looking at some frozen foods. She knew them from the time when one of their sons played hockey.

As his wife got close to them, they turned to face her. The mother put her hands on her hips and gave the nastiest, most horrible glare. The twins stood there giving evil glares as well. His wife gave a pleasant "hello" to which they said nothing but continued to glare.

This type of treatment continued on until her health was being compromised. She was also having bad dreams or not sleeping. They knew that if they were going to be in any shape at all when the time of the trial came around, something had to change.

During Easter vacation of 1999, they went down to the Branson/Springfield area of Missouri. They knew this area of the country fairly well. Here they set a fleece before the Lord.

Armed with about twenty-five resumes, his wife spent their vacation applying for a job at the various schools. Several schools granted her an interview right on the spot.

There were two schools that seemed to have some potential for hiring her. When they got back home, she prayed that if they were supposed to move, God would send only one school to her. She did not want to make any mistakes. She wanted Him to make it obvious.

They were ready to accept whatever God's will was. They would stay in the heat of things, or leave their family and move to Missouri if that was what God wanted.

One day at School, she received a phone call from a very southern sounding man. It was the Middle School Principal from the Forsyth School District. She had all she could do to not turn cartwheels. This was the job she had secretly hoped she would be offered. Needless to say, she accepted.

She kept this all quiet until she had met with her Superintendent and the School Board. At the Board meeting, her Union Representative presented her request. They all seriously thought the Board would grant only one of the three years that she had requested. After all, that was all they had done for anyone else.

They were all very happily surprised when the Board granted her a leave of absence for three years. They did this after the Chairman asked her if she would promise to come back at the end of the leave. His wife agreed to this.

In June, they went down to Forsyth to get ready for the move. In that time, they bought a van to use to move their belongs. Now they needed a house.

The realtor showed them all kinds of places. Most of them should have had a match taken to them; they were in such bad shape. Others were simply out of their price range.

Time was flying quickly. The fellow at their motel suggested that they look at the mobile home a friend of his had just listed. A mobile home was the last thing they wanted. They put him off as long as possible and then finally agreed to at least go look at it.

When they got there, they were greeted by a lovely couple. The mobile home was in better condition than anything else they had seen. It was also completely furnished, right down to the pots, pans, and bedding.

His wife knew immediately that was the place for them. Finally, Dewey heard the same message from God and by the end of the week they had a home. God is a miraculous God. They now knew for sure, this was exactly what they were supposed to do.

In August, they moved to Missouri and his wife started her job and took on a class at the University of Missouri Springfield.

Dewey was able to get a temporary job working for the Lawrence Welk Complex as a host. He loved that job.

When this job ended he worked in a retail confection store. What was so refreshing was how kind everyone was. The boss told him what a good job he was doing.

He and his wife met many God fearing people. They would just come over to them at places like Wal-Mart and start talking about JESUS.

They also experienced complete freedom to come and go as they wished without any thoughts about what the people they met would think about them or say to them. That included going to Church.

Going to Church in their local area had become impossible due to the number of Church people that decided to believe the rumors and lies instead of finding out the truth.

In Missouri, they were able to visit any denomination they wished without any harassment. Going to Church was where a lot of healing took place. Worshipping through the songs, the sermons, Bible readings, and prayer times helped develop a peace in their hearts. **These things brought healing to their wounded spirits.**

When they got down to Missouri, they were away from the harassment and pressure of the community. They were able to settle down and listen to God.

One idea that God brought their way was to do a Prayer Letter. They sent out letters to all Churches in the Moose Lake area as well as other areas of the country where they had connections. People were asked to sign up to be prayer warriors for them in their battle against the false allegations that had been levied against Dewey.

Soon they received a response from Dewey's army buddy's Church in Indiana. Everybody in the Church signed up to pray, even kids. There was also an individual from New Jersey who responded. The Church where one of their sons attended also was praying for them.

These were the only responses to their Prayer Letters that they ever received. There was not one church in Moose Lake that responded and all Churches in Moose Lake were contacted. They never called or asked about the situation. Without hearing anything from all these Churches, they had to assume they refused to pray for them.

GOD knew what Dewey needed to start recovering from the damage done by the School and people of Moose Lake. He sent Prayer Warriors from outside the Moose Lake area and the many people they met in Missouri to encourage them.

- 30 -

THE TRIAL BEGINS

Dewey had to sell over half of his equipment to pay legal fees. He had a contingency contract with his attorney, but he still had to pay a retainer fee and court costs. In all it amounted to about fifteen thousand dollars.

By this time, his attorney was getting very difficult to work with. At first, he was eager to represent Dewey and wrote many eloquent documents on Dewey's behalf.

Then it became apparent that he was getting offers of money to get Dewey to settle out of court. Dewey made it clear to him that he would not settle.

The attorney sent him a new contract. He wanted to get paid hourly instead of the contingency fee contract they had. He claimed that he lost the contingency contract so they needed to make a new one. What a liar!

Finally the day came when his attorney called to tell him that a court trial date has been set. Dewey was glad, but his attorney was sad.

He was being offered more and more to get Dewey to settle out of court. The School did not want to go to court at all.

Dewey tried to get a new attorney but no one would do it. Dewey had no money but he had a million dollar lawsuit that would be decided soon. He found himself stuck with an attorney that desperately wanted to settle out of court so he could get his bribe money. Remember, this is the man they discovered could not speak in public. This was a very scary situation.

The closer they got to trial, the more desperate his attorney became. He was calling Dewey every fifteen minutes telling him that he was going to lose. He finally just hung up on his attorney.

When his phone calls did not work to intimidate Dewey into settling, the attorney sent over night letters that cost a mint.

One day the attorney called to tell him to give it up. Dewey said, "You know Petey, when this is over I'm gonna write a book."

Wow! He said, "I'll sue you."

"Are you scared the truth will come out?" His attorney hung up.

The only way to restore his honor and reputation was to have a jury vindicate him.

The day arrived and they went to trial. The Judge threw out four of the five charges against the School. Dewey knew at that point that nothing was in his hands.

His so called attorney, who had been hired and promised to represent Dewey, whispered in his ear that they could settle now. He said he could call an adjournment. He told Dewey he could get maybe ten thousand dollars. But they would have to do it now. The attorney was really desperate to get out of going to trial.

Dewey informed him that he would take his chances. He turned away from his attorney but he still kept babbling at him about settling.

The trial was taking place in Federal District Court in Duluth, Minnesota. The presiding Federal Judge was the Honorable Judge Mildew.

It turned out he was a "dishonorable" Judge. He was the youngest Federal judge appointed to the bench by President Bill Clinton.

The first day of the trial involved jury selection. There was to be nine jurors. Three were picked by the defense, three by Dewey, who was the plaintiff, and three by the Judge. There were about twenty people in the jury pool from which to pick. They came from many different towns in a two hundred mile radius from the Federal Building in Duluth.

Dewey and his wife were shocked. His attorney had no clue how to pick a jury member and showed no interest in helping them. The Judge allowed Dewey's wife to be at his side for the trial. He and his wife picked their three jurors. Their choices were based on the opposition's questions since his attorney refused to ask anything important of the jurors.

At last it was time for the trial to begin. The first witness called was the Superintendent of the Moose Lake School, Dr. Moldy. His attorney was warned three times by the Judge to stop wasting the court's time.

It was obvious he was throwing the case. He must have been bought off. Why else would an attorney make himself look so inept in front of a judge, jury, and one of his peers?

He would not ask any important questions such as: Why she would suspend a driver when he had a legal passed drug test? Basically all he did was stand in front of the court and look at the floor or ceiling, wasting the court's time.

The way his attorney was wasting time with questions that had nothing to do with anything important, it was clear he was trying to sabotage the case.

When Dewey's witnesses were called, the opposition attorney grilled them in detail. He was actually better for Dewey's case than his own attorney.

He had Dewey's wife testify on the finances of the farm. He asked her why they had to sell equipment for the advertised price. She explained that it was because that was all they could get.

The attorney then made a profoundly ridiculous statement that could only make sense to the judicial system.

"When I advertised my house for sale, I had people come and offer me more than I asked for. "

To this his wife said, "Well, we didn't have a lot of people lining up to buy a 1978 Ford farm pickup."

Even the jury cracked a grin. No one could tell, from watching the jury, where they were leaning and there were still several days left of the trial.

Dewey finally told all of his witnesses to not depend on his attorney to ask pertinent questions about what they had seen or heard. He told them to just be bold and say what you saw or heard, even if not asked.

Dewey's wife even wrote up a set of questions for each of their witnesses based on what they knew. When his attorney first got the questions, he acted happy. However, as the trial continued he just put the questions on the lectern and never looked at them.

In spite of this, Dewey's witnesses did an excellent job. He was so proud of these people. They just got on the witness stand and spoke their mind. The reason they did so well was that they told the truth. There were about twelve witnesses for Dewey.

One of the most difficult of his own witnesses to hear was his son. He and his wife had moved into the farm to oversee it in Dewey's absence. During this time, his son was a witness to some of the School's shenanigans.

When his son and his wife came home from shopping one day, they discovered a note on the door of the house. It was taped wide open on the door. Anyone who came to the house that day was able to read the contents of this note.

The note instructed Dewey to go to the local clinic at a certain time to retake the drug test. This was a definite violation of data privacy laws.

During the testimony, his son told about the effect the School's false allegations had on his Dad. As he spoke he became very emotional and broke down as he shared that he felt that he had lost the Dad he knew and loved so much. The only dry eyes in the court room belonged to the School's attorney, Dewey's attorney, and the Judge.

The trial continued. Dewey thought that if they showed the jury exactly what setting up the sample looked like, it would help them understand. He brought a beaker of water and an actual specimen cup like the ones that they used for giving a drug test.

He explained and showed his attorney how to demonstrate pouring. He showed that if he held the cup at a slant, it would give the wrong amount for a reading.

The School had kept changing their story about what happened. They were trying to figure out ways they could "misinterpret" that law to prove Dewey was guilty of something.

One of their schemes was to say that Dewey had not provided a large enough specimen for the sample. This demonstration would have proven their theory wrong. Dewey's attorney refused to do it.

To help the jury see some of the most important documents, such as his drug test results, he ordered copies of these documents printed on three foot by five foot sheets of evidence paper. They were readable from forty feet away. These were put up in the court room early in the trial. The jury looked at these daily.

Dewey also got an overhead projector to show the same evidence on the screen. While he was setting up the projector, they noticed that it was their daughter-in-law who was struggling with the projector screen. She was in the very early stages of labor but his attorney did not lift a finger to help her. How disgusting! Dewey's wife spoke very loudly to the attorney to get his attention and tell him that he should be setting up equipment, not a pregnant woman. Finally, the attorney helped. (By the way, she had the baby the very next day!)

Neither attorney knew how to operate an overhead projector so Dewey did that himself.

He even let the School's attorney use his evidence. The man did not even realize he was sinking his own ship.

Dewey had never seen anything like this before. He was on edge. Both he and his wife watched the proceedings very carefully.

His wife had just had knee surgery a few days before the trial began. She was still in a lot of pain. However, Dewey's attorney was so ill prepared; she had to sit right next to him to help find the documents as he needed them.

One day during some testimony, they noticed Judge Mildew slowly bowing his head. They thought maybe he was looking for something on the floor. Then they realized that he had fallen asleep. At some point later, he jerked to attention with eyes wide open like saucers. He just stared at the School attorney. It was quite the sight!

Another time they watched the Judge as he sat gazing across the court room. Suddenly he leaned back so far; he almost tipped his chair over. They learned then and there the reason Federal Judges refused to allow cameras in their court rooms. They cannot risk having the public know what they are really like in the court room.

Bart never looked at the jury when he gave testimony. Somehow, Dewey's attorney caught him in a lie on the stand but he never pressed charges of perjury against him. The specimen taker lied on the stand also. Their testimony in court was the opposite of what they said in their depositions. Dewey's attorney never elaborated on that at all.

One thing Dewey's attorney did do, was that he gave Bart a copy of the drug testing rules given by the Moose Lake School for drug testing. Bart couldn't read it. The attorney had to help him with just about every word. When they finally got done, he asked what it meant.

Bart said, "What what meant?"

"What you just read."

There was a long pause. All eyes were on him as they waited for a response. He finally admitted that he really was not sure what it meant.

There were many times that Bart had no clue what to say. He tried to look around Dewey's attorney to see the gestures that the Superintendent was giving so he would give the answer the School wanted him to give. This was pointed out to the attorney, but he did nothing about the School's obvious coaching of a witness.

On that day, they all found out that the person who was overseeing the drug testing, the bus Supervisor, could not even read or comprehend the rules. But not a word was said about that. It was as if his attorney could not embarrass the poor little boy.

There was a real good reason Bart shook like a leaf. He had to remember all the lies he made up in the past.

A cousin of Dewey's wife was in the gallery watching the proceedings. A question was asked about the number of doors on Dewey's house. As she listened she realized that Bart was lying. Bart was saying there was a screen door and then the regular door. He claimed that he taped the notice containing data private information on the inside door. She had been to the house and knew they had only one door on their house.

She also discovered a piece of information that proved interesting during the rest of Bart's testimony. Every time he lied, he turned beet red from the neck up. They informed Dewey's attorney to watch for that, but of course, he ignored this and never pressed Bart on any lies.

When Bart's testimony was over, the Superintendent spoke directly to the Judge and asked if she could be excused from the rest of the trial to visit friends in North Dakota. Judge Mildew did everything but lick her shoes. He was so apologetic for wasting her time. Of course she was allowed to go.

"I will also be going hunting out that way so we hope to have this wrapped up in a few days." said the Judge. It was sickening to see how they gushed over each other.

The testing lab gave extensive testimony on Dewey's behalf. They had a special person that gave court room testimony all over America.

This was the very first case of its kind in America. Where would there ever be charges rendered against a person for having a negative drug test? It was appalling to the testing laboratory in Chicago that such an accusation had been made. They were very willing to help Dewey.

The School attorney was getting to the end of his rope with the testimony of the lab. It was all in Dewey's favor. To show his desperation, he asked if there were trains that passed nearby the testing lab or heavy trucks hauling loads that could have upset the drug test causing Dewey to have tested positive.

"No!"

The questions were tiring and long. Their only purpose was to wear down the jury so they would quit listening. Did it work? Did they get bored and stop paying attention?

The testimony from the testing lab left no question in the minds of the jurors. Dewey had given a large enough sample. It was a proven fact that if the sample was not adequate, the lab would have thrown the sample away, as per Federal law, and requested him to provide another sample.

When the lady from the testing lab was asked who owned the sample, she stated that the donor owned the sample. The School does not own the pee sample.

Dewey was the last witness to be called. After his attorney questioned him, he was interrogated for hours by the School attorney.

Before the trial had even started, Dewey had to go through fifteen hours of grueling testimony for his deposition. Over and over again, the School attorney asked the same questions but phrased them in different ways. Since Dewey told the truth the first time, all of the answers were the same. That's the way it was during the trial also. The attorney was deliberately trying to trip him up.

The flat out lies that 'ole boy came up with were purely disgusting. In his desperation to discredit Dewey, he said that Dewey could never get along with the people in the Church that he used to attend because he was so controversial.

The School attorney was talking about the fact that Dewey and his wife had left their Church over ten years before. Dewey's attorney sat at the table as if he was a spectator to the court proceedings.

Finally in disgust, Dewey's wife nudged his attorney and told him that was old history and had nothing to do with the case. That was the only time Dewey's attorney gave an objection for anything and it was on the grounds of separation of Church and State not "relevancy".

Since Dewey did not believe there was such a thing in the American Constitution as the separation of Church and State, before the Judge had time to say anything, Dewey said he would be glad to answer the allegation. He looked the Judge square in the eye.

He said, "Go ahead."

Dewey said, "We had been doing a good job of ministering to the people in the area and the Church was out growing the facility we were in. The preacher suggested adding on or building a new church. That started a fifteen year firestorm. Half of the congregation wanted to do something and the other half did not want to do anything. We thought it was time to move on, so we went to a different Church."

Dewey always gave his answer directly to the jury. He would look them in the eye. He believed that a person could tell who the dishonest people were because they cannot look someone in the eye. So, when he looked at the jury, they would know he was telling the truth.

When Dewey was on the witness stand he had plenty of time to observe Federal Judge Mildew. He noticed that the Judge's eyes looked dilated.

As a bus driver, he had lots of training in spotting drug abuse and reporting it to School authorities. There was one case on his route that was really bad. It was dangerous.

The boy should have been charged with a felony, so said the Principal. But when they brought the matter to the Superintendent Ricky, he said he did not want to do any thing that would embarrass the School. Nothing was done as usual.

As he sat in the witness seat, the red, flared nose and the eyes going all over the place made him very suspicious. The Judge sure fit the bill. And he had absolutely no ability to concentrate on the proceedings.

The only time in ten days that Dewey's attorney shined was when he gave his closing remarks to the jury. This was a time when God totally took over the court room. He put words in the mouths of both attorneys they would never normally say.

His attorney said, "Picture a feather pillow being opened to the wind and blowing to the east, the west the north, and the south. That is what these false stories all these years from the Moose Lake School have done to Dewey."

He also went on to quote Proverbs 22:1 "A good name is to be chosen rather than great riches, and favor is better than silver or gold." This proved that a reputation should be greatly valued. The Moose Lake School had ruined Dewey's reputation and he would most likely never get it restored.

It was amazing how calm and collected Dewey felt. He had no fear. He felt good and the reason was due to all the prayers by friends and family. The outcome of the trial was totally in GOD'S hands. Dewey knew that GOD had put His words into his attorney's mouth at the very end of the trial.

Then the School attorney got up to speak. GOD spoke through him as well. He opened his remarks to the jury by saying, "Dewey was an honest man before this trial and Dewey has been an honest man during this trial."

Wow! Dewey didn't know the School's attorney was on his side! He was sure the man did not even know he said that.

The rest of his talk to the jury was not even understandable to the Judge. It was all convoluted gibberish.

The jury got its orders late in the afternoon and went to deliberate. They first had to decide if the School had allowed data private information out to the public. If the answer to that question was yes, they had to decide on the money award.

The Federal security officers were kind to Dewey and his wife while they waited for the verdict. They had a strong sense that they were hoping he would win. They had been in the courtroom for most of the trial and knew all the evidence that was presented.

The Duluth News Tribune was covering the trial. The television stations were there. However, the two newspapers from Moose Lake, The Star Gazette and The Arrowhead

Leader, never ever showed up or even interviewed him any time before or during trial.

All these people knew Dewey and his family personally. Why do you think they would not ask for his side of the story? Following the trial they used plenty of type for the School.

The next day, the jury brought their verdict back to the court room. Dewey and his wife tried to look at them to see if any of them would give a hint as to what they had decided. All nine were absolutely poker faced.

Waiting for the verdict to be read, was nerve racking and emotionally painful. They had been told by his attorney that if they lost, they would most likely lose the farm. The tension mounted as they waited. Which way would it go?

No matter how much you trust God, it is difficult not to have some doubts at times like these. As they waited, they prayed. Their family and one of the bus families sat right behind them. They could literally feel them praying.

The wait seemed endless. The tension was mounting and they felt sick. The moment finally came.

The foreman was asked for the verdict. He stood up to read it. **The Moose Lake School was guilty of the charges.**

In fact, on one count Moose Lake School was the very first in the state of Minnesota to be guilty of that charge. The jury said it was a flagrant miscarriage of justice.

The look on the face of the judge was unbelievable. He was so mad at the jury's verdict, he shook. It was like a surprise to him that they could find the School guilty. It was as if he was saying, "How dare you?"

What he did say was, "I have never ever polled the jury before but I will now." He asked each one of the jurors questions about whether the decision represented their true feeling that the Moose Lake School should be found guilty.

All nine answered with a resounding and emphatic "YES!"

It was finally over. Dewey, his wife, family, and the bus family made it out to the hallway. Here they met up with members of the jury. Now they were all smiles and giving words and hugs of congratulations.

They revealed that it had taken only one vote to determine whether the School was in the wrong. They unanimously agreed that this had been a conspiracy to defame, demean, and destroy Dewey's good reputation.

They stated that the thing they spent the most time considering was how a whole community who knew Dewey could just stand by and let this happen to an innocent man.

They were also appalled that the people from the community were not even interested enough to fill the court room to see what would happen.

The Federal agents congratulated him. Since they heard all the evidence, they had a feeling that the jury would see the truth and come up with this verdict. They just could not say anything before this time.

The Judge was mad. The jury was glad. And Dewey and his family went home with great relief that, it was over. Or was it?

The jury was made up of just about all professional people, teachers, a DNR man, and business owners. He could not thank them enough for toughing it out those ten grueling days of trial.

His friend, Harold, came over to the house that evening to hear what happened. He was so happy about it. They were making plans to go back to working together.

Dewey still had a lawsuit against Bart, the Supervisor, in Carlton County Court. That was a lock tight case with some of the same witnesses as in Federal Court.

Unbeknownst to Dewey, the courts started their conspiring again. This was probably instigated by Dewey's attorney who was trying to charge the court for exaggerated expenses. He tried to double and triple charges. He would call Dewey up all excited about what he was going to charge them.

For Dewey, it was never ever about the money, although it would be nice to have some for what they put him and his family through.

The jury awarded Dewey around one hundred and twenty thousand dollars. This was the highest award that had ever been given in the state of Minnesota. His attorney was so excited that he started acting very childish. He acted like it was a "done deal."

Dewey's wife kept reminding the attorney that the School had a right to appeal but he denied that they would do this.

About five months later, upon the request of the School's attorney, Federal Judge Mildew rescinded the jury verdict. He felt that the decision of nine honest people was out weighed by the opinion of one person, himself! This was outrageous!

The Judge took Dewey's life away forever as far as his reputation in Minnesota. The people were so gullible. Or perhaps, they just needed a permanent whipping post.

Well, Peter Rabbit scampered away as fast as he could. Dewey interviewed a couple of other lawyers to see if they would take the County Court case.

Then he met another attorney. This attorney professed to be a Christian. He even prayed when they met.

Dewey asked him if the case was to ever go so far as the Supreme Court, would he be willing to go that far.

"Absolutely! You have a lock down, open and shut case."

Dewey was in Missouri at that time. The new attorney would call and say that he had this hearing and that coming up. He also said that Dewey did not have to be there.

Pretty soon he found out that the County Judge threw out the county case against Bart. He also discovered his appeals court case against Judge Mildew was thrown out.

The next step in the Federal case was the United States Supreme Court. He gave his new attorney a call. He told him, "I'm ready to go to the Supreme Court are you?"

"Yes. I'm checking on how to do this since I never spoke to the Supreme Court before." Dewey didn't hear from him for quite a while so he called him. He assured Dewey that he was still working on it.

Then it got so hard to get a hold of him. Phones were disconnected. He moved.

Finally after many weeks, Dewey must have surprised him when he was able to get his number. Dewey said, "Well when do we go to the Supreme Court?"

"Well I was talking to some of my lawyer friends. They said a bus driver will never get into the Supreme Court. You are not important enough."

Dewey said, "Maybe you should get some new friends."

The Judge from the Carlton County Court was a graduate of Moose Lake School so Dewey supposed he had a close tie to his almamatre and wanted to protect them. After all, what could justice have to do with anything?

To stab the dagger in a little deeper, the School sent Dewey a bill for all the court costs.

- 31 -

LAWYERS & THE ILLEGAL SYSTEM

YOU WILL NEVER FIND A MORE DISHONEST GROUP OF PEOPLE. My attorney and I met with the Union lawyer from Minneapolis. We met at a restaurant.

The Union attorney spread out his papers and we were in deep discussion when the waitress came over to take our order. It was noon and very busy.

He said, "We'll order a little later."

Sometime later she came back and said, "There is a conference area in the back and you can order from there. It is made for conference meetings."

There were people waiting for a table and I suggested we go to the conference area. I was ignored by both attorneys.

We were asked again, very politely to move as the waitress makes her money at this high point in the day. The bad part was that when our meeting was over, we just left. No meal was ordered and no tip was given.

A week later, I had a meeting with that lawyer at his office in Minneapolis. If you are a Bible believing, God fearing,

Jesus loving person you would surly have felt beyond a doubt that you were in the presence of Satan.

The first thing the lawyer said was how proud he was that he used the restaurant as his office and it didn't cost a dime. He asked, "Did you see the look on that waitress's face when we left? Ha, Ha. Ha."

This is a man that represents the A.C.L.U.

The up front fee for a lawyer is $1000, $1500, $5000, or $ 10,000. His fee is the most important part of the whole case.

You should know that lawyers are the laziest people on the earth. They don't even trust each other.

If you have hired a lawyer, you can expect that if you meet with him and he gets a phone call from someone, you will pay for the time he is on the phone with the other client. That person also pays. So the lawyer jokes with his friends at the end of the day about how many double pays he got that day or week. They used to bet on who would win but there was so much lying about it they quit.

They will count every minute they spend talking to you. The cost for every phone call will at least be five dollars. A thousand dollars can be gone in a day and if you want him to do more, pay now.

The object is to bleed you until you have no more. They have no remorse about leaving you high and dry half way through your problem.

Now what do you do? You do what over ninety percent of litigants do. You give up and the guilty go free.

Remember, guilty people don't care what happens. They know they have got it coming but if a court appointed lawyer can get him off, well good. Guilty people usually don't get on the stand to testify for themselves.

There is a reason that the justice system moves so slowly. They purposely go slow so the person either dies or gives up.

The Constitution of America guarantees a swift trial. Don't ever believe that these judges are over worked. They spend a greater amount of time on the golf course and on vacation.

If you are an honest person and need to go to court, ask your attorney if he believes in TV cameras in the court room. Ask the judge if he believes in cameras in the court room.

If he does not believe in cameras in the court room, it is because he is a dishonest person and does not want the public to see him at work. He has something to hide.

There is so much dishonesty in the court. It is amazing we still have America. The courts and judges have taken the rights of the people away.

The proceedings should be tape recorded, because a court stenographer makes too many mistakes. Leaving testimony out or putting the wrong word in changes the meaning of the testimony.

Of course money speaks. If you don't think there is a great deal of under the table money, you are a very ignorant person. You should read the Constitution for yourself. Don't let others tell you what it says.

- 32 -

LESSONS LEARNED

That was then, and this is now. Dewey and his family had been through a lot. As you go through life and its trials, there are lessons to learn if you want to take the time to learn them. Many people do not. That is a shame.

During his legal battle and the time following, he learned a lot about God, other people and himself. As unpleasant as it all was, these lessons were important.

His faith in God was confirmed and became even stronger through it all. He knew God loved him before the legal problems, but now he was impressed with just how much he was loved.

Other people said he was given a "Job" experience. Dewey learned that just as God tested Job way back in Bible times, He tests people today too. God tests us to see if we will stand or fall. This testing also strengthens a person and prepares one for future situations.

As Dewey daily searched the Scriptures, he had found his strength to endure his situation with the School. It had been tough but God had been faithful to His Word. He walked beside Dewey and when he could no longer walk, God had carried him.

Not only was the legal situation a test for Dewey and his family, it was a test for the Church and the community. A great number of people had known him for years. He learned a lot about them.

Most of them found it much easier to just believe what the School said about him. They did not call or ask to hear his side. Anyone should have known that there are always two sides to every issue, but they did not want to hear his side. They might be lead to "do" something and they did not want that.

Some people that he thought were close friends did not believe all the rumors, but they did not let Dewey know that they were on his side. Apparently, people thought he was clairvoyant.

When a person is going through hard times, the only way he knows that others are on his side, is if they say something. Christians need to understand that it is their responsibility to stand beside one another in a very present way and uphold their brothers and sisters in the faith.

He even discovered that one person from the Church had deliberately given information to the School's attorney that was not relevant to the case, but could put him in a bad light. Christians should not treat other Christians in this way. If Jesus was standing next to that person would she have still said those things? Not likely. We are to live our lives as if Jesus IS standing next to us because HE IS.

Thankfully, he found a few brave and faithful friends that were willing to walk through this valley of darkness with him. It was interesting to look at them and see exactly who they were. They did not go to his Church. Their children had ridden his bus as had many others. Some of his supporters were not even believers, they just knew right from wrong. They knew that there was no way that he did what the School was accusing him of doing and they stepped to the plate to help.

The community of Moose Lake was being sorely tested and they failed the test. The biggest questions the jury had during their time of deliberation were, "Why did the community let this happen? Why didn't they speak to the Board members? How could they just sit there and let this happen to a good man?"

It is easier to believe a lie, than to go investigate and find out for yourself what the truth really is. It is easier to sit in your house and do nothing but hope for the best. There were others who were simply thankful it was him and not them in the hot seat and they were not going to do anything that might call attention to themselves and change their safe comfortable lives.

There were people who saw and heard what happened but they refused to testify. They were scared for their jobs. Their refusal to do the right thing tore friendships apart and put riffs between relatives. Some are still dealing with the choices they made.

His friend, Harold, said it was a wonder to him how these spineless people who had jelly for a backbone, could even stand up. It was difficult for him to put himself out on a limb for Dewey. It was hard to get on the witness stand. But he did it because it was the right thing to do!

These people will need to search their own souls and be responsible for the choices they made. Will Dewey and his family trust them or other people in the future? Not for a very long time.

There was one thing Dewey saw happen, but was puzzled about. How could a whole community embrace a newcomer to that community, such as the Superintendent, and not question anything she did? How could they let her run rough shod over people who had lived in the community most of their lives? How could they let an outsider disrupt the lives of so many good, decent people?

Dewey also learned things about himself. He learned that he had his limits. When you are young and strong, you think you are invincible. You can do anything. But when you are attacked by Satan, it does not matter how strong and able you are, you need more than just yourself to make it.

Dewey surrounded himself in Scriptures and confirmed to himself his beliefs in God were real. They were genuine and strong. He learned that he could overcome things not thought possible before – with God's help.

He would cling to his favorite verse, John 3:16. "For God so loved the world He gave His only Son, that whosoever believes in him should not perish but have eternal life." If God loved him enough to let Jesus suffer and die on the cross, he knew God loved him enough to help him through the false allegations.

Dewey learned that if you do what is right and trust God, He will honor your obedience. He lost a lot in his battle with Satan and the Moose Lake community. However, the blessings far out weigh what he lost.

Dewey was asked if he would like to be a security officer in Missouri. In his mind he thought he would never qualify with all of the false accusations the School made against him. He never told them about having to go to Federal Court.

Finally, after several weeks he decided to take the steps necessary to be a security officer and let the chips fall where they may.

He did not know if the School had made their accusations known to the Federal government. Going through this process was a good way to find out.

He passed the Missouri Sheriff's Association test. He passed the FBI background check. He passed all the written and oral tests given to become a United States Security Officer.

He was assigned to be a security officer for a hydroelectric dam. He was given a uniform. In one year's time he achieved the rank of second in command. Shortly thereafter, he was offered the job of Commander. He enjoyed his position immensely.

It was ironic that he worked in the heart of the worst drug infested area of the country. The Ozarks had even beat L.A. County, which usually ranked first.

God had blessed him with time out of the heat of the situation so he could get back his sanity and his strength. His family had been kept together. So many times, when times get hard, families fall apart. With God's help, he had built his family on God's principles (on the Rock) and when the storm came, they were able to stand together.

God is good. He is faithful to His Word. He loves us at all times and in all circumstances. He is all powerful.

Dewey also learned many things about the justice – or rather – the injustice system. He learned to expect lies from both attorneys. Judges are not always fair and unbiased. They do succumb to bribes and payments under the table. Just because the evidence is on your side, there is no guarantee that you will win your case.

Remember the statement "You are innocent until proven guilty?" That is not true. The lawyers and judges laugh about this one. You are guilty until you can prove you are innocent.

He found out that it is best not to give a deposition. The opposing attorney will use your deposition to confuse you by twisting your words. They try to make it look like you do not know what you are talking about or that you are lying.

He also discovered how good the opposing attorney can be at cutting you off when you are getting to the truth of the matter. They really do not care what the truth is. They just want to win.

An honest person does not have any trouble looking people in the eyes when they speak. All of his witnesses looked right at the jury when they spoke. They were all telling the truth. The School's witnesses either looked down or looked at the School attorney when they testified. They had to figure out which of their lies fit where. They had to be sure to cover up their secrets. They could be distracted by looking at the jury; they had to focus on what they had said before so they could keep their testimony straight.

A truthful person can look anywhere and still accurately give their testimony. You see, the truth does not change. It is what it is!

Another thing Dewey learned was how important it is to document everything. Even in daily life, it is good to keep a record of what happens. Record the time, date, people involved, and a detailed description of the event. Make copies of your documents in case something gets misplaced, lost, or stolen. This is especially important in certain workplace settings. You never know when you will be the victim of a false allegation.

He learned that you should not give original copies of documents to your lawyer. He will most likely lose them.

Many people think that because they pay Union dues, that the Union will automatically back them up. Dewey found out that they are better at representing guilty people than innocent ones. They are not particularly interested in an individual. They are looking out for the larger group.

You do have a right to representation from a Union, you may have to be bold and let them know there will be consequences if they refuse to represent you adequately.

A lawyer's goal is to get the case settled out of court. He will do anything in his power to get this to happen.

Even though you have paid an attorney to represent you, many will take bribes and just pretend they are on your side. They have only one side and that is their own side.

If you are truly an honest attorney, judge, principal or superintendent, we apologize for the global statements that have been made. Please do not take offense. We have not met you yet.

Dewey's hope is that you can realize that as Christians living in today's society, you may be a target for a situation similar to his. He hopes that the hints he has given will help you prepare in case you find yourself in this kind of situation.

Do not give up on God, the Bible, or prayer. They will be your strength and get you through those difficult times. Remember what is said in Romans 8:31 "…If God is for us, who is against us?" No matter how difficult or dark a situation may be, you can count on God to be on your side.

You can also be encouraged by Philippians 4:13 which says, "I can do all things in him who strengthens me." When God is walking beside you or carrying you, it is amazing what you can do.

So let the lessons Dewey learned help and encourage you as you walk through this journey called life. Keep your eyes on Jesus and you too will make it.

EPILOGUE

The story that you just finished is based on the actual events and situations that my husband has experienced. Everything really did happen.

However, through the years one's memory tends to get a bit "foggy". Some items may be slightly out of order. This does not change the situation or the effect that these events had on him.

You may have noticed that some names were a bit unusual. The names of the evildoers have been changed. But God knows who they are!

I am sure that by now you have discovered that Dewey and I are a team. We look out for each other and try to help each other when the going gets rough. We strongly believe that God brought us together as Christians and marriage partners for that purpose.

During our early days, money was tight. We lived very frugal lives. I worked out until the children started coming. At that point we decided I would be a "stay at home mom."

I have never regretted that decision even though it meant less money coming in. It meant home cooking instead of eating out. In fact, when I hinted that I wanted to go out to eat, Dewey would offer to help carry the food outside!

As we raised our boys, we worked together. We supported each other's parenting decisions. This gave the boys a unified front. They could not play us against each other. We love our boys.

I have to say that as they grew up, they gave us no major problems. We enjoyed all of the activities they engaged in and learned a lot right with them.

Today, our boys are all grown and married. They have awesome jobs and are very hard working people. They have chosen wonderful girls for their wives and we could not be happier.

We are so proud to say we are Grandpa and Grandma. I love to watch Dewey with the kids. His sense of humor and love for them really shine.

I was your typical small town girl. I could not tell one end of a cow from the other. When we looked at the herd, Dewey would point out the bull. At first they all looked the same to me – big and black. I finally learned a few things to look for and that helped a lot.

When Dewey was hunting for a wife and met me, he was not so sure I would fit in. To make sure, many of our dates included farming adventures.

Here went this prim and proper "city girl" out to help with fencing. Of course, the day was wet. So much for the glamorous look! I soon discovered that I would do just about anything to spend time with Dewey. So I traded in my cute, flirty outfits for something less sophisticated that would let me get down and dirty.

One of the times I am the most proud of as far as farming goes was when I pulled a calf all by myself. I have to admit, I was scared to death. I thought back to what Dewey and I had done together. I hooked the chain on the calf's feet and held on, hoping the cow would not decide to get up again! Then I planted myself in a hole in the snow that I had made.

On the next contraction, I started pulling. And pulling. And pulling!

Finally out popped the calf. Both the mom and I just laid there in the snow. Then I grabbed the calf, took off the chain, and dragged the calf over to the mother. She just laid there. I thought, 'Oh, Great! She's not getting up! She's not even licking her baby. What to do?"

Thank goodness, I was able to get a hold of a farmer friend who helped get the mother up and everything turned out fine.

The most difficult thing I have ever had to do was to watch Dewey go through dealing with having false allegations made against him.

It was scary to have most of our friends turn completely away from us or ignore us. We really found out who our real friends were. It was disappointing.

We learned after time, that what the School meant for evil, God meant for good. We also learned that even though we did lose a lot, we were also greatly blessed.

During this we lost most of our "so-called" friends. Dewey lost his job as a bus driver and all of his custom hay baling customers. He lost his retirement. His cattle and much of his equipment had to be sold to pay the lawyer. I lost some of my seniority at my job. We both lost our faith in mankind. Our health declined.

However, our blessings included new friends in Missouri. Wonderful jobs and a great little place to live in Missouri. God brought us a new business of manufacturing soybean candles. We started out with about a dozen fragrances and with God's help, we now make over two hundred fragrances. We have our very own website at Showmecountrygifts.com. God has blessed us financially in ways we could never have imagined.

We still have our three boys, but now we also have three daughters (in-law) and four grandchildren. Our faith in God has grown by leaps and bounds. There are so many blessings; it is hard to count them all.

Did you notice that the blessings out weigh the losses? I believe that when you stand up to evil, and look to God for your direction, He will honor your obedience.

Our hope by writing this book is that you, the reader, will realize that evil is all around us. What happened to Dewey can happen to anybody. You could be next.

We want you to know that you can make it through the dark valley. If you need a prayer partner, contact us through our website and we will stand in the gap for you.

But most of all, never give up on God. Listen to Him. If He says stand up and fight, be brave and do it. God will be right there with you.

For now, May God bless you Real Good. Keep your eyes on Jesus and we will meet you at Heaven's Gate.

~ Dianne